Emily
Moonlight

D1738062

B. Andrew Scott

DEDICATION

For Huff, our first misunderstood "monster."

Emily Moonlight

ISBN 9781978009820

Cover art by Enrique Meseguer

This book draws loose inspiration from Native American Trickster and shape-shifter mythology, however it is in no way meant to be a direct representation of Native American culture or traditions.

The author has great respect for Native American and First Nations people and cultures, who have been under and/or misrepresented is most artforms. Which is why the protagonist and title character is intentionally of Native American blood.

CONTENTS

ACKNOWLEDGMENTS

Thank you to my family for your patience, even my kids who aren't allowed to read this yet. To all my readers and listeners for your unfailing support.

To Stephen King for *Silver Bullet*, Joe Dante for *The Howling* (and my dad for taking me to the drive-in to see it when I was far too young), and Michael J. Fox and the cast and crew of *Teen Wolf*. You all helped create my love of werewolves and my vision of them as more than just monsters.

And Len Wiseman for reinventing them in *Underworld*.

Chapter 1

Portales, New Mexico was a typical college town on the eastern border of the arid state, just a stone's throw from Texas. It was a community of modest ranch houses with gravel lawns and brick walls for fences. Much of its population of 12,000 souls was comprised of the faculty at Eastern New Mexico University.

Adam Morrison had never been big on the party scene, but he'd officially given up late-nights sixteen years ago when he and Lorie adopted their oldest child –

a baby girl they named Emily Grace. On top of that, Adam had been teaching 8:00 AM classes, five days a week, for years. So the last place he would normally be found at 1:38 A.M. on a Tuesday was driving up and down the streets of Portales in a blue Honda minivan with the headlights turned off.

And yet, there he was.

Adam rubbed his eyes and pushed up his glasses. He sipped

on a Coke he'd grabbed from the fridge on his way out the door to keep him awake. Twenty minutes earlier he'd been sleeping just fine. Until the sound of his teen daughter's squeaky window being pushed open woke him. Of course, she was long gone before he even made it down the hallway.

This was happening more and more often. Adam had jumped out of bed and pulled his well-worn Cubs hat over his wild blonde bedhead, and pulled his emergency duffle bag – the one secured with a padlock – out from under the bed.

Lorie hadn't heard him. She was still sleeping peacefully, her dark brown hair covering her face. Good, Adam had thought. Better she didn't sit up worrying.

Dr. Adam Morrison was a tenured professor of chemistry and introductory biology at the college. Originally from the Midwest, Adam had completed his undergrad work at UNM in Albuquerque, a few hours west of Portales, and fell in love with the Southwest. Shortly after meeting his wife Lorie in grad school, he took a job with ENM and they settled in Portales where they'd stayed for nearly 20 years.

This could not keep happening, Adam thought for the thousandth time as he drove. The town was too small. Adam had even caught wind of rumors that the local police were calling in assistance, arranging for more roving patrols at night. Emily was putting herself in serious danger, whether she was aware of it or not. It was well past time he got his daughter far away from this place.

For a fleeting moment he again imagined how a change of scenery might somehow make a real difference - even change her. But reality swept it away from his mind like just another unrealistic daydream.

Emily's problem was far more serious than one of simple geography. She needed real medical help. But even as a scientist, Dr. Morrison had no idea what the solution could be. There were no specialists for this. Whatever the answer, he was committed to doing anything to protect her.

That was the silent vow he took the day the adoption official first placed her in his arms. His hair was blonde and his eyes blue, while her hair was black as night and eyes nearly as dark, but it made no difference. She was his, regardless where she'd been born or to who. Their bond was instantaneous. The moment he held little Emily, he *was* her daddy. She was his little girl. And he'd stop at nothing to save her. That was the role he willingly accepted in that moment.

So that was why he turned the van down 1st street at that late hour, and saw the yellow lights of the Shell station, and the red roof and white neon of the Taco Box facing it on the other side of the street. There was always quite a bit of drug activity around the area. Something told Adam he might find his daughter there tonight.

It was a long run from their house, but she could make it easily. He peered into the darkness for any sign of Emily. She would be hard to miss. But what Adam Morrison didn't know was that his daughter had already been to the restaurant, gotten what she was on the hunt for, and fled further into the night.

Todd Ryan and Jeff Peterson were Seniors at ENMU. They were both from affluent families in Santa Fe, but didn't have the grades to get into Ivy League schools. And after a handful of Hollywood celebrities went to prison for bribing their kids' way into prestigious universities, the boys' parents refused to help them coast through life any longer. They had no other option but Eastern.

They pledged Kappa Sigma because they heard it had been Jimmy Buffett's fraternity when they were tailgating in an amphitheater parking lot one summer. That seemed like a logical choice for two ne'er-do-wells like Todd and Jeff.

The two Polo clad blue bloods had barely stayed sober long enough to see their senior year. Now exams were upon them and they needed to pack an entire semester into a week. They also had a spring festival to organize, including trying to book Snoop Dogg to perform.

This meant there would be no sleeping for a while, and that required chemical assistance. The boys had met a townie shooting pool at a local bar who said he could hook them up.

They'd been told to meet the guy behind the Taco Box at 1 AM. When the police would eventually arrive and find Todd Ryan's hand, it would still be clutching a wad of twenty dollar bills he was handing to the dealer. The rest of him would be lying about 10 feet from it.

Dr. Morrison slowly pulled around to the back of the white brick *taqueria*. It was of course closed and locked up for the night. There was no one around to see him. But when his lowlights fell upon the dumpster, he saw a grisly scene. But sadly, not an unfamiliar one anymore.

A ginger college kid – Todd Ryan – whose body was contorted like a horseshoe. Along with missing a hand, his throat had been completely torn out. His rib cage had been wrenched open and his remaining organs were strewn all over the crumbling asphalt.

Adam didn't know the young man's name, but he paused to think of his parents. No matter what the kid had been up to in this neighborhood in the middle of the night, Adam couldn't help but feel a swell of pity for his folks. They would be receiving a horrific phone call.

An older Mexican employee had apparently stayed late to clean up and waited to take the garbage out on his way to his bike, locked up behind the building. It was common to see men like him, riding bikes around town late at night. They were usually saving as much money as they could from these low-paying jobs in order to send it to loved ones back home.

Unfortunately, in this man's case, his efficiency turned out to be his last mistake. His face had been practically ripped from his skull. Another victim whose face was mashed into the asphalt was splayed, spread eagle. His shirt had been torn away to reveal demonic tattoos and symbols on what flesh was left on his body. His spine had been pulled out through his back.

Even though he'd seen it before, Dr. Morrison winced at the excruciating scene. He felt his stomach turn. A voice in his head hoped, whatever the young man had done in his life, he'd already been dead when *that* had happened.

There was no sign of Emily.

Adam knew she only had a few minutes left at best. He turned off the lights and rolled out of the lot and back onto the street. Sooner or later someone would discover the gruesome scene and the police would be called.

As it was, there might have been security cameras from the gas station pointed that way. He knew, as a respected, and frankly, *white* college professor, his alibi of looking for his runaway daughter would probably hold up. Even if he were to be identified at the scene and the police wanted him to come in for questioning, he'd go willingly.

He had no DNA under his fingernails. No blood in the car. They'd quickly determine he had nothing to do with the murders. No simple man could have committed this horrific crime.

Morrison pulled back onto 1st Street and drove north until he reached Cherry Street, where there was an empty grass lot that had once been a park, and a gravel yard across the road. As if an answer to prayer, there she was. Emily was lying naked in the middle of the lot.

Adam hastily put the van in Park and started to open his door. Something slapped at his passenger window, causing him to jump in his seat.

"Help me man!" a desperate voice cried out.

Adam looked and saw a young man with spiky brown hair and half his face clawed up and bleeding profusely, banging on the glass and leaving bloody handprints. He would later read the kid's name was Jeff Peterson.

His other arm, what was left of it, was wrapped up in his yellow Polo shirt. Dark, wet blood had completely soaked through most of the material.

"Please sir!" the young man cried again. "Help me! Please!"

"What happened?" Dr. Morrison asked calmly, rolling down the window.

"Some bitch," the Peterson kid started. "She went fucking nuts! Turned into a monster. She fucking attacked me and my buddy! Oh shit! I think Todd's dead! I know it sounds crazy, but it's true! Please, help me! Take me to the hospital! I'll pay you!"

"Was anybody else with you?" Adam asked.

"No . . . no, man, just me and Todd," he answered. "Alright, look, we were buying some pills. We know a guy who deals back there."

"Just weed usually, I swear. He dead too, man. This bitch walked up. We . . . we asked if she was okay. Then she turned into this fucking *thing*. Like a movie. Like a real werewolf! She bit off my fucking hand! Please, help!"

"I believe you," Adam said calmly, sliding his hand into his duffle bag. He had two choices. "Can you even see me with your face like that?"

"Barely man," the kid sputtered. His good eye was full of tears mingling with blood from his face. "I think I'm blind on one side now. Shit, man! I can't even feel my eyeball! Please help, mister!"

"I'll do what I can," said Adam.

He wrapped his hand around the handle of the Titan SM6088 anti-riot pistol. At least he hoped he'd chosen the right one. It was a black handgun with an attached CO2 cartridge.

In one fluid motion, he quickly drew it from the bag and fired a rubber pellet directly into the young man's forehead. The kid stood there stunned for a second. Adam pulled the trigger again, blasting another slug into his head. Finally, Jeff Peterson dropped to the street.

Adam Morrison put the van back in Drive and cranked the wheel, driving up over the curb and onto the sidewalk. He ran to his daughter, who was still lying completely out cold in the dewy grass. Her dark hair was matted with sweat. Her hands and face covered in crusted blood. He wrapped her with a blanket and cradled his teen daughter in his arms.

"It's okay baby," he whispered. "Daddy has you. Daddy always has you." With a quiet groan, Adam lifted her up and carried her to the van, laying her across the backseat.

"We'll be home soon. It's all over. You're safe." At least he hoped so.

Adam grabbed the glass cleaner and a rag out of the back of the van and quickly washed the blood off the passenger window. He'd do a better job tomorrow, taking it through a car wash a few times. He drove his daughter home in darkness, grateful to not pass a single other car on the road.

Once they were safely in the house, and he was convinced they hadn't been followed, Adam cleaned Emily off in the shower while she barely made a sound.

Her condition, brief as it usually lasted, completely sapped her of all energy. Emily would sleep late tomorrow for sure. When she woke, she'd only have fragmented memories, as always.

He helped her into a t-shirt and flannel pajama bottoms and tucked her into her bed as if she were four years old again. He leaned over and kissed his daughter's forehead.

"I'm going to fix this," he assured his sleeping daughter for what seemed like the millionth time. "I swear to God, I will find a way."

Dr. Adam Morrison slowly shuffled back up the hall to his own room. His mind was numb. He was well aware that at such close range, even with a less lethal weapon, he may have killed that young man tonight. At very least, the kid could have lasting brain damage.

But the other option inside the bag had been an unregistered .38 revolver, and that one did not fire rubber bullets. At least he had given the boy a chance at survival.

If he did recover, he'd have to explain the dead drug dealer and his buddy, and the innocent Taco Box employee, not to mention his own missing hand. Adam wasn't too worried about Jeff Peterson leading the cops to them.

It didn't matter. Emily was all that mattered. Adam Morrison said he'd protect her at any cost. That was his job. If that meant killing some frat boy who'd been buying drugs behind a taco joint in the middle of the night, so be it.

They'd been at this for over a year now. Emily would slip out of the house and he would go after her. Not to stop her of course. Adam had learned early on that there was no stopping her when she changed, and it would only endanger him, or the rest of the family.

When this thing overtook her, he had to let her feed. His job was to follow close behind and get her out of harm's way when it was over.

When this demon left her body, and his daughter fell to the ground, Adam would be there to scoop her up. And woe to anyone who happened upon her in that state, even if by accident.

That was why he always took his special bag, for those "just in case" scenarios. Adam hated what he'd become. He didn't even recognize himself anymore. All his life he had despised guns, and yet he'd been forced to purchase and use two in the past year. And so far, he'd gotten away with it.

He had always thought of himself as a moral man. But fate had erased the lines of traditional morality for him, and his family. He couldn't risk witnesses who might make more problems for his daughter.

Adam rationalized his actions by telling himself most of Emily's victims had been "bad people." The only kind of people who would be on those streets in the middle of the night. Most of the time, the police weren't all that motivated to look too hard for answers.

But he also couldn't deny that there had been a few instances of seemingly innocent people – like that poor worker tonight – who'd simply been in the wrong place at the wrong time. The school teacher whose dog needed a late night walk. The insomniac computer programmer who'd gone for a walk.

Fortunately, Emily's victims were often written off as animal attacks. Cougars, coyotes, wolves; all seemed reasonable in this area.

"Is she okay?" Lorie stirred and asked when he finally got back into bed sometime around 3:00 AM.

"Yes," he whispered, kissing her on the head. "She's fine. She's in bed."

"What about you?" she asked.

"I am how I am," he answered with a sigh. "Had a close call. It's good that we're getting out of here. This town keeps getting smaller. I don't think we could keep this game up much longer. And I can't wait to get into that lab in Charleston."

Chapter 2

The island of Lune de Sang, South Carolina was officially founded by a wealthy French merchant named *Levasseur* in 1817. It was long rumored that some of the scattered crew of the notorious pirate Stede Bonnet had hidden on the island while their "Gentleman" captain swung from the noose in nearby Charleston.

Monsieur Henri Levasseur, it was said, had arrived from New Orleans under mysterious circumstances. He was described as a thin, well-dressed man with skin that was corpse white, and long, straight black hair cascading from under a top hat. In every portrait he was shown wearing opaque spectacles.

The enigmatic Levasseur arrived to his new island home with many servants of all colors, none of which ever spoke, according to local lore, and a pretty young girl rumored to be his daughter.

It was Levasseur who gave the island with its foreboding moniker – christening it the "Island of the Blood Moon" –

and who built the first of many antebellum mansions that now dotted its coastline.

The dirt paths of Lune de Sang were replaced by cobblestone streets and gas lights as rich merchants and pirates alike, tired of the perils of life along the trade routes, continued to arrive, building their mansions on the backs of slave labor. It became clear to the likewise wealthy community of Charleston that there was money on Lune de Sang, but from where it came, none dared to ask.

Another mystery about the residents of the island was that for many years, they didn't bother to build a bridge to connect them to the mainland. Supplies, building materials, and laborers were ferried in on tenders from big ships anchored at sea. It would be nearly two centuries before a bridge was finally built to connect them to Charleston.

Rumors about the small isolated community were salacious and exciting. The most common, which had endured for over 300 years since, was that the day Monsieur Henri Levasseur appeared, the death toll and reports of missing persons around Charleston began to rise exponentially.

There were numerous wild theories floating around Charleston dinner parties. Levasseur was a serial killer. Levasseur was a phantom. Levasseur was a vampire. Levasseur was not even a real person, but a myth created by a cult. Levasseur trafficked with the devil himself.

Only one of those rumors was actually true.

Over time the pirates and traders disappeared, and Lune de

Sang became an eclectic mix of doctors, artists, lawyers, and socialites. The only common bond among the residents of the small island was money. Some old money, some new, but the vintage of your fortune was overlooked, so long as you had one at all.

Lorie Morrison, born Lorelei Marie Delaney, came from an old money family in South Carolina. The Delaney family had made a fortune building ships in the 1700's. They took big hits during the depression, and again after 9/11, and the 2008 real estate crash.

But there was still a little money left when Lorie's father died, and not many heirs to fight over it. Her dad managed to leave her a small inheritance, and the family's house on Lune de Sang.

Lorie had never wanted to live on the island again. She'd spent many summers there as a kid, but said she didn't have many memories of those days. As she got older and wiser, she began to hate the pretension, and what she called the "gossip culture" of the island. Everyone smiled at everyone else, but verbally assassinated them as soon as they were out of earshot.

Beyond that, she just never felt comfortable there anymore. Too many ghosts, and too many demons, she would sometimes say, and then dismiss the comment when pressed.

When she'd inherited the house a few years earlier, they'd considered selling it straight away. A house on the island would fetch millions; a nice windfall for them. But her husband had advised patience. Adam often said it could be their retirement plan. Or at very least a nice vacation home.

That was well before the problems with Emily began. Now the mansion she'd never wanted seemed like a Godsend. Perhaps it was recompense for the shitty hand fate had dealt their daughter.

Lorie was well acquainted with tales of bayou culture, voodoo, and occult activity from the Gulf to the Carolinas, and on down to the Caribbean. She knew all about inexplicable secrets. But one subject she didn't have much of a background in was lycanthropy. After all, werewolves were seldom brought up in pleasant conversation.

In fact, while Lorie Morrison believed there were strange things lurking the corners of the night, she had seldom given the werewolves a serious thought. Not until the night she and Adam discovered their daughter tearing a homeless person to shreds behind the high school.

After that, she began to read everything she could find on the legendary monsters. Books on werewolves, shapeshifters, Native American tricksters – Emily had Navajo blood after all – anything even close to the subject that took it at least somewhat seriously.

Lorie would sometimes stay up late into the night searching occult websites and studying werewolf lore. Most of it was just silly, she told her husband.

"Isn't all of this silly?" he asked with an exhausted smile.

"Yes, I know," Lorie had answered. "But give me a break. Some of this stuff is on the same level as killing vampires with garlic. I think I might have more luck when we get to Lune de Sang. My family has books stored in the attic that go back a lot further than these."

"Do you honestly think your family kept a book about Emily's condition?"

"I don't know," she sighed and ran her fingers through her hair. "Most of them were written in Europe, centuries ago. But still, they might shed some light."

The Morrison's didn't know much about Emily's family, or her people. All they knew for sure was that at least one of Emily's biological parents had been of Navajo descent. Beyond that her family history, her lineage, it was all a mystery. She'd been abandoned at a church as a newborn. At different times, they'd both wondered if her birth parents had some inkling of Emily's *disposition*.

They never called it by the common names. Werewolf was simply the "W word" around their house, and they tried not to use it if they could avoid it. It was a silly word made up for horror stories.

This was real life. It was just some kind of medical anomaly, Adam had said.

Lorie's husband had chosen a more academic stance when it came to his daughter's current plight. If this condition - lycanthropy – was real, then as a man of science, Adam reasoned there had to be a scientific explanation. Some genetic switch that could, perhaps, be turned off. Maybe it was a virus of some sort. That idea he could work with.

If the problem was cellular, the solution - if there was one - would have to be as well. At least those theories seemed more reasonable to him than something supernatural.

As fate would have it, in the midst of figuring out what to do about their daughter and how to find a cure, Adam had received a call out of the blue regarding an opening at the Medical University of South Carolina.

It was a prestigious research school that, as fate would have it, was located essentially just across the bridge from Lune de Sang.

According to her husband, they'd said he would only have to teach one class per semester, and he could devote most of his time to research. Adam would have one of the most celebrated laboratories in the nation with the newest state-of-the-art equipment and facilities at his full disposal.

It was everything that Eastern New Mexico University was severely lacking. And he could lead his own projects. In other words, Adam could work on whatever he wanted, without interference from the administrators. The truth was, their offer seemed like the definition of *too good to be true.*

Of course, he would have to pull double-duty in an attempt to develop some kind of side project he could talk about in meetings, and pass off as justification for his presence, while he primarily worked on helping Emily. But that didn't matter now.

Together, the couple opted to leave New Mexico and move east. Hence the reason they loaded all the possessions they wished to keep, along with Emily and their 8 year-old human tornado of a son named Grant into their dark blue minivan and made the cross-country trek from arid New Mexico to balmy, swampy South Carolina.

Emily had been adopted, but Grant had been a biological surprise. The normally hyper-active boy was sound asleep when they crossed the bridge from Charleston that led into Lune de Sang.

His spikey hair was mashed against the window, a piece of red licorice hanging from his law, and his fingers still gripping his tablet with the thick blue rubber childproof casing. He'd already managed to de-childproof two cases before it.

Emily gazed out her side of the van, earbuds in tight, listening to My Chemical Romance. She hadn't spoken much over the three day road trip. She hadn't minded leaving New Mexico. She didn't have friends there anyway. But it felt weird moving to someplace so different, so strange, from anything she'd ever known.

She was also well aware they were moving because of her.

The van bumped along the cobblestone coastal avenue, passing enormous antebellum manors with alabaster columns and spacious porches. Tall palmettos dwarfed the houses lining the sidewalks.

One particular pink bricked, four-story mansion with a wraparound two-story porch caught Emily's eye. Not for the architecture but for the brick columns out front, grown over with flowering ivy and a wrought iron gate.

Emily's gaze was broken when she realized she was being watched as well. She could literally feel the gaze of the young black woman with the wild curls wearing a sleek gray cocktail dress with a plunging neckline. She was leaning against a column on the porch, smoking a long, thin cigarette, watching them drive by with a curious smirk.

Emily quickly looked away, but something kept pulling her attention back to the strange woman. She squirmed in her seat as she saw the girl's eyes following them the entire way, sipping a glass of dark red wine – despite appearing to be no more than a few years older than Emily.

"You okay sweetheart?" Emily's mom asked, turning around in her seat to look at her daughter. Lorie's eyes followed hers out the window.

"Oh, yeah, a local. I guess the warnings about smoking haven't quite made it to the island. This is tobacco country sweetheart. You'll probably see a lot of it. When I was a kid, everybody smoked. It's so gross."

There was something strange about her mother's voice, Emily thought. She was rambling. And her eyes never left the girl on the porch as she talked.

Finally the pink house and girl began to shrink out of view. Lorie shifted and turned to face forward again. Emily looked back and watched the young woman walk back into the house.

She couldn't say why, but Emily had felt a strange, anxious

sensation. It was tingling up and down her spine. Hopefully their new house was nowhere near this street. Given the size of these places, and her parents' income, she figured the odds were their new home wouldn't be anything like these. Emily was wrong.

"There it is," her mother announced. They had turned a corner only a mere block away from the strange girl in the pink mansion.

"Which one?" Grant asked, popping right up like a Whack-A-Mole game and scrambling to lean between the front seats. "Which one is it?"

"The blue one," their mom answered. "Right there, with the yellow shutters."

It was a narrow, three-story square affair with two columns holding up the entryway over the front door. There was no gate at the sidewalk. Just untrimmed hedges which opened up at the brick walkway.

"Cool!" Grant proclaimed. "Does it have a pool?"

"No," Adam said. "No pool buddy. But we're a short walk from the beach. Or bike ride."

"The beach," Emily spoke, wistfully. It suddenly occurred to her that she'd never been to a beach. She'd never even seen the ocean. She been so preoccupied staring out the window at the island, she hadn't bothered to turn her head to see the sprawling Atlantic to the right.

"Yes honey," said Lorie. "It may not be oceanfront, but our

house is only five minutes from the best stretch of beach on the island."

Emily used to dream of the ocean. Of lying in the sand, watching dolphins play in the surf. She'd lived her whole life landlocked in the desert. This was indeed a new world.

For a moment, she dared to feel a sense of hope. If dreams could come true, however small, then maybe nightmares could be ended.

Chapter 3

Sophie Broussard had been amused to see the funny family car driving along Saint Charles Boulevard. They didn't get many sensible vehicles around there. Mostly expensive Bentley's, Mercedes, or Rolls Royce, along with the occasional collector's item like the McAllister's Aston Martin coup.

All manner of ostentatious machines to signify the drivers' wealth and disregard for the value of a dollar. But Sophie had been completely caught off guard by the teen girl in the backseat.

When they locked eyes, sirens began to ring out in her brain. An electric chill surged down her neck into her spine. Her instincts told her something unusual had come to Lune de Sang. Something that could be bad for her.

Then again, she shrugged as she'd taken a final drag off of her cigarette, it could be fun too.

She took a sip of wine as she watched the van turn onto Saint

Ignatius Boulevard. She dropped her cigarette into a half-finished martini someone had carelessly left outside and returned to her dinner party.

"I apologize for stepping away," said Sophie, reappearing in her long dining room just off the main entry of the mansion. A half-dozen guests in dinner attire sat at the table waiting to dig into their salads.

They were all rich, older socialites of the island. The McAllister's were there, who made their family fortune in textiles over a century before. Mr. George Emmerson McAllister was a lecherous old man who liked to swill double gin & tonics, and to stare at Sophie's ass when she shuffled by.

While Sophie didn't welcome McAllister's gaze, she couldn't quite blame him either. His wife Rose resembled a sweet potato in a wig that put her lipstick on in the dark.

The La Becks had come from a long line of molasses runners who'd cashed in long ago and came to the island for legitimacy, spreading their millions into various industries and investments, and building many of the gaudy, newer *McMansions* on Lune de Sang.

The La Becks were at once celebrated and despised. Sophie tolerated them as she must, but their constant offers on her family home were growing tiresome.

Mr. Rodney La Beck had an orange spray tanned face and an overly toothy smile, like a gameshow host. His gray hair was always well-coiffed, and he was fond of wearing pastel shirts and matching pocket squares.

His wife, Luanne La Beck was tall and thin, with a pinched nose on which rested spectacles with blue lenses. Her hair was short and spiky, and an unnatural shade of magenta, and her face bore the constant expression of smelling something unpleasant.

Carol Anne Hendricks, the second most eligible bachelorette on the island, after Sophie, was there. Carol Anne was a 40-something ginger haired trust fund baby from Mobile with the temperament of a longshoreman and the taste for rum of a pirate.

She was quite possibly Sophie's favorite person on the island - almost like an immature, inappropriate aunt - and Sophie insisted Carol Anne come to every dinner party.

Lastly, the La Becks had invited their new realtor friend, Amman Griess. He'd only been on the island a few years. He was friendly enough. Couldn't be much older than late-thirties, but was said to have made a killing in Manhattan real estate before choosing to slow down in Lune de Sang.

Sophie had seen his picture popping up on park benches and yard signs; tan skin, deep brown eyes, and well-groomed shiny black hair. It didn't look like his early retirement was working out.

There was certainly something charismatic about him. Sophie even felt a slight strange attraction to him. She was never sure how that sort of feeling would pan out. There was a reason she lived alone in this giant house. Alone, that was, save for

Luther, who she always introduced as her *assistant*.

Luther looked like he belonged in a motorcycle gang. He wasn't exceptionally tall, but he was broad, like a tank. He wore a tight (often too-tight) white dress shirt and a black leather vest over his massive body. He was covered in tattoos, as displayed through the white sleeves usually rolled about halfway up his tree trunk arms.

A long braided ponytail of thick dark hair ran down his back. He had a long, thick beard, also sporting a single braid down one side, adorned with a silver Nordic hammer pendant.

The skin of his face was like wind whipped leather. His sausage fingers were adorned with heavy silver rings featuring skulls and monstrous faces.

In truth, Luther was her everything: her driver, her body guard, the *majordomo* of the house, and the closest thing she had to a confidant.

Luther seldom spoke to anyone but Sophie. Though he was often seen about town, driving a beastly black Ford F350 pickup that barely fit through the narrow streets of Lune de Sang, running errands, and picking up groceries and supplies for Sophie, among other clandestine chores she required of him.

Most locals crossed the street to avoid the hulking brute. He served every meal and, it was believed, even cooked them. One other strange fact was that Luther was never seen without dark black sunglasses over his eyes, regardless of the time of day, or whether he was indoors or out.

Luther pulled her chair out and Sophie slid into it at the head of the table. Her guests lifted their forks and began to eat. Sophie picked at a tray of charcuterie in the middle of the table.

"Aren't you having a salad?" old man McAllister asked in his phlegmy southern drawl, noticing she had no plate before her.

"Old Sophie's not one to waste room on rabbit food," Carol Anne said with a laugh, grabbing for her own martini.

"It's true," Sophie nodded, practically sucking a piece of prosciutto from her fingers. "I'd rather just eat the rabbit."

"Oh my," Mrs. McAllister exclaimed, almost choking. "That is, uh, this salad is divine. The herbs are so fresh. And the goat cheese tastes as though you made it here. It's to die for."

"*We'll see*," Sophie mumbled between smiling teeth. She lifted her wine goblet. "Speaking of, . . . Luther?"

Her dutiful servant stepped forward from behind her and grunted.

"I could use another drink while we wait for the main course," she said.

"Maybe you'd prefer to drink it *straight from the bottle*," he grunted at her. "Cut out the middle man." Luther briskly swiped up her glass and disappeared down the hall. They could hear his heavy boots fading away toward the kitchen.

The dinner guests were all shocked at the manner in which this servant had just spoken to his boss. Sophie laughed heartily. She grabbed a handful of olives from the tray and leaned back in her chair.

"What?" she asked, seeing her guests staring at her as if waiting for a reaction. "Oh, Luther has been with me forever. We're like brother and sister, and bicker like it too. But he does anything I ask, so he's allowed to be snarky."

"So tell me, Miss Broussard," the newcomer, Amman Griess spoke up from the other end of the table, "how long have you lived in this spectacular home?"

"This old place?" she asked, looking up at the chandelier over the dining room. "It's alright."

"Must be an awful lot of upkeep," Mrs. La Beck said, peering over her blue glasses.

"Well, it can be tough to keep after the cobwebs," Sophie said. "The good news is I'm not afraid of spiders. They know better than to bite me."

"This is her family's home," Carol Anne offered.

"I was told it once belonged to the founder of the community," Griess said, sounding surprised. "A Mister *Levasseur*?"

"You heard correct," Mr. McAllister added.

"And you are somehow related," Griess said to Sophie. "Are you not?"

"That is what they tell me," she said, shifting in her seat. "Can't tell you the exact branch of the family tree, but they gave me the deed. You know, legend has it *Henri* liked the ladies, and he planted his flag in many mounds between New Orleans and South Carolina. White sand or brown didn't matter. It's possible I'm related to half the island, but Lord knows they wouldn't want that to get out, so I get to keep the house without any trouble."

"Oh, well," Griess stammered sheepishly. "It's certainly a beautiful home."

"Miss Broussard controls property rights for some of the finest beachfront property on the island," LuAnn La Beck said, with thinly veiled disdain in her voice. "She's been gracious enough to allow the residents to make use of it at no charge."

"Ah," Griess reacted approvingly, half raising his glass toward Sophie.

"Provided the land is never developed of course," Mr. La Beck said, disapprovingly at first, but realized his lack of etiquette and winked at Sophie with his alabaster smile.

"That's correct," Sophie said matter-of-factly. "It will always be that way."

"Always?" Mrs. La Beck added. "Well, I'd think eventually you will receive an offer so sweet even you can't turn your nose up at it, regardless how much money you're already sitting on."

"He's right Sophie," old man McAllister chimed in. "It's just good business. The resort proposal would secure a comfortable future for you, and your children, your children's children. Sure, it doesn't seem important now, but believe me, nobody stays young forever."

"I'd argue otherwise," Sophie muttered. She gave a kind nod towards the new guest. Then she glared at the others. "I suspected you all wanted to have dinner for reasons beyond just introducing me to Mr. Griess, charming as he is." She nodded to the new comer.

"This discussion is getting so old," Sophie continued. "As you've no doubt noticed, George, these hips haven't coughed out any children. And the last thing this island needs is more tourists. There are plenty of resorts in Myrtle Beach. Haven't you all got enough money?"

"In time you'll learn how foolish that question is," said Mrs. McAllister, sipping her martini.

"You have no clue what time has already taught me," Sophie replied, popping an olive into her mouth.

"You sure can be frustrating sometimes, Miss Broussard," Mr. McAllister chuckled.

"Why is that?" Sophie asked. "Because I won't let you all build tacky hotels on our beach? Or is just because I'm a young colored girl in an $8 million dollar mansion, and it frustrates you that I have the power to deny your requests? To the land, and to my ass."

McAllister went red and started coughing as he choked on his romaine. His wife looked irritated and slapped him on the back, trying to dislodge the lettuce from his windpipe.

"Well, I believe that to be of such firm resolve at such a young age shows remarkable integrity," Griess said. "It's inspiring."

Sophie eyed him awkwardly before nodding with a forced smile. "And where is it you have come to us from, Mr. Griess?"

"New York," he answered coyly. "But I was born in Egypt. That was a long time ago. Manhattan is where I studied and learned English, and fell in love with this new world."

"I love New York," said Carol Anne. "What the hell brought you to a backwater swamp like Lune de Sang?"

"I would hardly call this magnificent island *backwater*," said Griess. "And that's a difficult question to answer. I suppose you would say I was ready for a new start. Something just called me to the area."

"Where do you live again?" Rose McAllister asked him.

"I purchased the white, two-story Colonial manor on Flor de Lis Ave," he nodded to the old woman.

"Oh, the old parsonage?" Mrs. McAllister asked. "Near the old cemetery?"

"Yes," Griess smiled, looking embarrassed.

Amman Griess was well aware rumors abounded across the island about the property. The house had been built in the late 1800's and had once been used by the adjacent church – Our Lady of Blessed Mercy – as a parsonage. There were rumors that the backyard had also been used by the church as an overflow cemetery.

Parishioners would be buried in the official graveyard behind the church for their public funeral, but once their families were gone, the priest would instruct the gravediggers to move them to an unmarked grave in the vacant lot.

Funerals were big business, even back then. Blessed burial plots came at a premium on the tiny island. As a result, it was possible the bones of dozens of corpses were rotting behind, and maybe even *under* the house.

While the stories were denied by the church and dismissed by the residents, a cross was installed on the cupola that sat atop the house, just in case. The hope was it would dissuade any angry spirits that might come seeking vengeance for disturbing their resting place.

Griess had the cross removed as part of his renovation. The house had sat in disrepair for a long time before the enigmatic, olive-skinned newcomer has purchased it. Now the house was once again considered a shining star of the island's real estate.

"Although I have been assured the legends are not true," Griess nodded politely. "There are no bodies buried in the backyard."

"Why did you take that cross down?" Mr. McAllister asked, seeming somewhat offended.

"I assure you, I meant no disrespect," said Griess. "However, it did not feel appropriate. While I consider myself directly connected to the spiritual world, I do not subscribe to any religion. I follow what you might consider an older faith."

"Amman will be listing the Carpenter's house at the end of Delisle Street soon," Mr. La Beck interjected, trying to change the subject and hopefully lighten the mood. "The white two-story at the end of the cul-de-sac. The house isn't much, but the backyard is beautiful, and it has a lovely swimming pool."

"That's right," Griess spoke up. "The owners, the Carpenters, had to move rather abruptly. I've been working feverishly to get it staged to show. And you are correct. That pool is the major selling point. The yard is very quiet and secluded. I believe if you threw a party, you might scream as loud as you like back there, and not a living soul would hear."

"Partied with some screamers, have you Mr. Griess?" Sophie smiled.

"Well, I've heard the Carpenters threw all sorts of sordid parties in that house. But of course that's none of my business," Mrs. La Beck gossiped between sips of her martini. "Terribly sad about their boy, though. He was killed in some terrible accident in California. What was his name dear? Michael? Jason?"

"Well, let's see," her husband thought. "Fred was the dad. Old Freddy and I used to play golf sometimes. They had three boys. It was the youngest that was killed. Wes, wasn't it?"

"That's it," his wife said. "Wesley. Odd boy. You know he moved out to California to work at Disneyland or some such foolishness."

"I think it was the Knott's outfit," her husband added. "No, that's not right either. Dinsmore's. Dinsmore's Adventure Kingdom. We took our children when it first opened back in the 70's."

"Well, whichever," she continued. "He was crushed by some sort of train ride or something."

"Crushed and burned alive," LuAnn La Beck added. "On Halloween of all days. Can you even imagine?"

"Lord Jesus," Carol Anne said, crossing herself and chugging her martini.

"And you think those places are supposed to be safe for children," LuAnn continued. "No thank you. I'll stay right here on Lune de Sang."

"What makes you think Lune de Sang is safe?" Sophie mumbled, picking at the meats on the tray. She looked up annoyed. "Where the hell is Luther with my drink?"

Luther had indeed gone to fetch her requested refill. Cooks in white jackets and hats were buzzing all around the kitchen preparing the night's meal. The smells of spices and roasting meat filled the air.

Luther usually did perform most of the cooking in the house. It was quietly a passion of his. He often thought if life had dealt him a few different cards earlier on, he might have been a chef. Maybe it would have kept him out of trouble. Who knew?

Tonight Luther was not preparing the food. Luther had hired caterers for this party, as he'd been busy the night before, stocking Sophie's private bar.

The kitchen which Luther had remodeled to Sophie's specifications was a wide open affair with a restaurant style range, two large stainless refrigerators, and a walk-in freezer.

Cooks were busy at their various stations, preparing filets, and risotto, grilled whole duck, and a pasta with seafood. Sophie insisted on variety at her dinner parties, and always a focus on proteins - usually on the rare side. Vegetarians would have to stick to salad and pasta.

"And as for any vegans," Sophie would say with an eye-roll. "God help them." If she didn't have the option of a cruelty-free lifestyle, why should anyone else?

Luther walked past the hired staff and into the walk-in pantry. The cooks from the catering company had been strictly instructed not to enter this area, as they were to bring everything they would need to prepare the meal.

The pantry was off-limits, and each had been tipped an extra $100 when they arrived as they were once again reminded of this rule.

Luther entered the pantry without turning on the light and shut the door behind him. A dim blue light illuminated the storage closet. He pushed against the shelving unit stocked with canned goods at the back of the pantry until it slowly rolled back with a click, and the entire unit slide sideways, vanishing into the wall, revealing a solid steel door behind it.

There was a black glass screen mounted in the door. He touched a meaty index finger to the panel and a red light began to flash. Luther lifted his glasses revealing too milky eyes which he opened wide in front of the sensor. The monitor beeped and the magnetic locking mechanisms inside released.

The heavy vault door slid inward with a whisper, revealing a secret room with plain concrete walls. The floor was scored toward a drain in the center.

Just above the drainage hole, a man was strapped to what could best be described as a medieval torture device. He was strung up about a foot off the ground, his arms stretched out as if being crucified, and his legs splayed as well.

There was a black bag over the man's head and his chest was shirtless. One arm was wrapped in gauze which was soaked through with blood.

When he heard the door the captive began to scream, but the gag in his mouth only allowed muffled cries inaudible to the rest of the house.

Behind him was a metal work bench of sorts where a black wine bottle sat out, uncorked earlier to let it breathe. It was a 2014 Chateau Lafitte Rothschild. It retailed for around $600 a bottle.

Luther looked inside the case that had arrived the day before. It had come with 12 bottles. There were five left, counting this one. Luther shook his head.

A large knife lay on the table beside the bottle on a folded black towel. The blade was wide and exaggerated with a serrated edge along the back. The handle was carved from jade and inlaid with a bronze coil wrap. Luther prided himself in his collection of ornate and exotic knives. He picked it up gently to admire the craftsmanship yet again, then turned to the business behind him.

"Take it easy," Luther said, gripping the writhing man's clean arm which tensed, unable to pull away. "The boss wants another drink."

Without a moment of hesitation, Luther jammed the point of the blade into the meat of the man's forearm and slid down, severing the Brachial artery. The victim let loose a tortured howl and twisted from the searing pain. Luther let him howl.

There was no chance of the sound escaping through those thick walls. It had been built that way on purpose.

Luther held up the wine glass just below the arm as blood flowed freely, like it was simply running from an opened spigot. He filled the goblet a little less than halfway, then filled the difference with Cabernet from the bottle on the table.

Luther set the glass down and picked up a hammer. He swung it hard against the man's skull who immediately fell silent.

"Back to sleep, little prince," he said. "Dinner will be over soon, and so will this bad dream."

Luther cleaned off his blade with the black towel, which he folded over and placed back on the table. He reverently set the knife back down on it, as if tucking it in for the night, and slipped back out of the room with Sophie's drink.

The door shut behind him and the shelves slid back into the place as he exited the pantry into the kitchen. The cooks made no notice of him as they were plating all the various entrees to be served. He carried the goblet back into the dining room where he immediately picked up on an uncomfortable silence.

"What did you say this time?" he grumbled, setting Sophie's glass down in front of her.

"It's about time," she said, pleasantly surprised. She took a deep breath through her nose, soaking in the aroma. "Mmm, my favorite."

"Enjoy it," he grumbled. "You've just about killed that bottle."

"Thank you, Luther," said Sophie. She took a deep drink from the glass. A rim of red stained her upper lip until she licked it away with a giggle. "Now that's better. Perfect temperature too."

"Thank you for your patience," Luther said, addressing the other guests. "Dinner is served."

Chapter 4

There wasn't a great deal of time for the Morrison's to settle in. They moved into their new home on Saturday and Adam reported to the university on Monday morning. Lorie took on the task of registering Emily and her little brother for school.

Lune de Sang had a small elementary school on the north side of the island so that task was quick and easy. It had been opened solely for children of the island's residents, to save their parents from having to cross the Sayle Bridge every morning. However there was no high school. Emily would have to attend Thomas Bennett High School in Charleston.

It was less than a mile and a half from the island, but like many of the streets here, there was no direct route. Most mornings Adam could drop her off on his way to work. Today he'd gone in early, driving his small Honda that they'd had the movers tow out from New Mexico.

Emily put on a black V-neck tee because her mom told her to "dress a little bit nicer than usual, for today." She also chose a pair of black nylons and denim cut-off shorts and stepped into her black Converse low-tops and climbed into the minivan. Grant was already in the back seat, watching YouTube videos of other spastic 8 year-olds playing video games.

The school was a newer two-story building on the east side of the Charleston peninsula, apparently named for a former governor. A sprawling white brick campus with a football field adorned with signs that read Home of the Bennett Bulldogs.

"Awesome," Emily said. "Another breeding ground for meatheads."

"Take it easy," her mother replied calmly. "You don't have to judge it so harshly just yet, *Daria*."

"Who?" Emily asked, annoyed.

"Never mind," Lorie smiled and rolled her eyes.

As they walked up the steps to the main entrance of the school, another girl about Emily's age was coming out. She was a few inches shorter, with thick, curly tendrils of auburn hair contained only by a maroon head band around her forehead.

She wore vintage cats eye glasses that were tortoise shell along the top and turquoise along the bottom. She was wearing a faded black t-shirt sported a white penguin in a top hat, and a billowy skirt of many colors. Her wrists were adorned with multiple beaded and woven bracelets.

She seemed to be burdened down by her hemp shoulder bag

stuffed with school supplies and new text books. She was looking at a paper schedule in her hand as she walked along, lost in thought, and absolutely not noticing Emily taking her in.

But then her head suddenly snapped up like a deer in the woods hearing a twig snap, and she immediately locked eyes with Emily.

The bohemian looking girl's eyes narrowed in a disapproving glare. They each continued walking in their separate directions, but they never broke eye contact. It made Emily very uncomfortable, kind of like the girl on the porch the other night, but this time she couldn't look away.

Within a few seconds they had each moved on and Emily realized her mom and Grant were already a few paces ahead of her.

"*Unbelievable,*" Emily heard the girl mutter as she walked down the steps.

Inside the school, the Morrisons met with the vice principal of Bennett High School, Isabelle Saunders. She was an older woman with thin jet black hair in a lavender skirt and jacket. She had no southern accent, making her seem glaringly out of place in the Carolinas. She had the nasal tone of a Midwesterner.

Ms. Saunders gave them a tour, seeming especially proud of the new auditorium. "I was something of a performer when I was your age," Saunders chuckled with a snort.

"Oh, wow," Emily raised her brows with feigned excitement.

Emily was sincerely impressed to learn the school also housed a large greenhouse for students to learn botany and horticulture. Rows of potting trays were lined up, waiting for the new term to begin.

Mrs. Saunders pointed out there was also an organic garden just outside completely maintained by the students who then donated all the produce to a local homeless shelter.

Okay, Emily thought, maybe it wasn't the worst school she'd ever been to after all.

"Well, now that that's over with," their mom said when they finally got back to the car, "what would you guys say to a little exploring? There's an area nearby called Heron Square that I think you'll really like, Em."

"I'm hungry," Grant shouted from the back of the van, feet up over the top of the seat.

"I believe they have food as well," Lorie called back. "But we are not going anywhere until you sit up like a human being and put on your seatbelt. You too Emily. Seatbelts save lives."

"Ugh, you're so corny," Emily muttered in the passenger seat. "It's not like it matters."

"Oh really?" Lorie asked her daughter through gritted teeth, hoping Grant wasn't listening. "Have we tested whether you're *car proof* or not?"

"Very funny," Emily responded, reluctantly clicking her buckle in place.

It turned out her mom was right about Heron Square. Emily quickly discovered it was in fact a cool little neighborhood in Charleston. It was solid city block of art galleries, thrift stores, funky head shops, small restaurants, bars, a coffee roaster, and an ice cream parlor.

There was art for sale everywhere; sculptures, paintings, and creations of metal and scrap that were beautiful and hard to describe. Murals had been painted all over the brick buildings and even painted on the sidewalk.

Emily loved the area at once, even despite her fear of swarming hipsters in tight pants and ironic mustaches those communities often attracted.

They settled on a tiny brick storefront restaurant on the corner called *PinkZZA*. It was a pizza place with no dining room but a number of small metal bistro tables outside.

The inside was entirely pink with shelves along the walls lined with pink poodle figurines and statues. The place smelled incredible, which made all three of their stomachs growl.

There was only a counter with an old fashioned cash register, a menu board filled out in multi-colored chalk, and a giant brick oven in the back that lightly wafted out delicious smelling.

A man with thinning bleach-blonde hair pulled into a pony-tail greeted them with a warm smile. He wore a pink tank top showcasing his ripped arms and a white apron covered in flower and spots of tomato sauce. His left ear lobe was distended from the weight of a collection of strange earrings.

"Well hello, beautiful family," he greeted them. "Welcome to PinkZZA! My name's Rafael. What can I cook for you today?

A few minutes later, the three of them sat at a table right out front to people-watch. Within ten minutes they had a large plain cheese, which was the only thing Grant would eat, and a salad and breadsticks.

Emily scoped out the street, taking in the sights and making mental notes of shops she wanted to check out when they were done.

"Not bad right?" Lorie asked after a few moments.

"The food?" Emily smiled.

"No," Lorie shook her head. "Not the food. Although this pizza is really good. Am I right, Grant?"

"Outstanding," he smiled with cheese dangling from his mouth and tomato sauce smeared across his cheek.

"I mean *this*," their mother said, gesturing around at the neighborhood. "This is nice, right? It's fun. The island isn't so bad either. I think we can make a life here."

"I wish it wasn't so hot," Emily said. "It's not even that it's hot. New Mexico was hot. The air here is, like, heavy. It falls on you as soon as you walk out the door. It's hard to breathe. And I feel wet. It's gross."

"Welcome to humidity, my little desert flower," her mom grinned. "I grew up in this stuff. It will relent a bit in the winter, but yeah, it's pretty much an all the time thing. You get used to it. I think."

Behind Emily's shoulder a man was about to walk into PinkZZA when he stopped, hand still on the door handle, and looked at their table. He let go of the door and approached them.

"Excuse me," he spoke with a slight accent. "I am sorry to disturb your lunch."

Emily recognized him in an instant from the park benches and bus stop posters she'd seen on every block the moment they crossed the bridge. He was a local real estate guy.

He was dressed in a blue suit with a yellow tie tucked into a gingham vest. He had a toothy smile, olive skin, and black hair slicked back into a wave at the nape of his neck. He held out a business card to their mother.

"My name is Amman," he said. He extended his hand. Emily noticed an ornate gold bracelet, as well as a gold pinkie ring. "Amman Griess. I believe you are new to the area, correct?"

"Actually I grew up here," said Lorie, shaking his hand somewhat reluctantly. She didn't want to appear rude, but was also wary of a possible sales pitch coming. "We actually have a house on Lune de Sang."

"Oh, yes, I know," he said. "I'm very familiar with it. It's a lovely home. It sat unoccupied for so long, I had hoped it might eventually become available to list. But I'm happy to see your family making a home out of it. I just saw your lovely family sitting here and thought I would welcome you to the neighborhood. Or I should say, welcome you back."

"Well that's very nice," she said. "Thank you."

"And what is your name little man?" Griess turned to Grant.

"G-money-rant," the rambunctious kid answered between bites of pizza.

"Oh my god," Emily muttered, covering her face.

"Grant," his mother exclaimed.

Griess laughed at the boy. He held out a fist for Grant to bump.

"Welcome to the hood, little homie," Griess said. Grant returned the gesture and Griess *blew it up*. Griess then turned his attention to Emily. He extended his hand.

"And what is your name, mademoiselle?" he asked.

"Uh, Emily," she answered as she reluctantly shook his hand. It was cold, but at least it wasn't sweaty like most people she'd met so far.

"It's a pleasure to meet you Emily," Griess smiled. "Are you enrolled at MUSC, or maybe the art institute?"

"What? Err, no," she smiled awkwardly, embarrassed, pushing her black hair out of her face. It was a little weird that he thought she was in college, but he suddenly seemed a bit cooler. Maybe it was just his lack of a *Gone with the Wind* accent. "I'm still in high school."

"You're kidding," he said. "I'm such an idiot. I shouldn't

have assumed . . .."

"Oh it's fine," Lorie said, trying to cover for him. "Believe me, she probably appreciated it!"

"It's cool," Emily smiled. "I'm going to be a junior at Bennett. Don't even have a driver's license yet."

"Well if you're ever looking to earn some extra money," he offered, "my office is always looking for help. We offer a paid after-school internship program. Not the most exciting place for a young person to spend their evenings, but I think it beats clearing tables at the island's endless fundraisers, like so many local teens do."

"That's an incredible offer," Lorie interjected. "We will definitely consider it."

"Yeah, uh, thanks," said Emily. She would much rather work a job and start earning her own money than go to school. She was never comfortable around other kids her age. And her condition was never an issue until the middle of the night so it wouldn't affect her ability to work.

"Well, I've interrupted your lunch long enough," said Griess, his gaze still hanging on Emily. "I just wanted to introduce myself and say welcome to the area. Again, if you need anything, you now have my number. Call me. Text me. I'm on social media. Whatever you prefer."

"Thank you so much," said Lorie shaking his hand again.

"Peace, Grease," said Grant, raising two fingers in the air as he tore at a slice of pizza.

"Master Grant," Griess bowed to the boy with a grin. He turned back to Emily. "And you as well Miss Emily. I am very serious. Don't hesitate to text me if you're interested in a job once you're settled."

"Uh, thank you," she said. "I will. Thanks."

Griess slid into his silver Mercedes parked up the block and drove past them, waiving as he did.

"Well that was really nice," said Lorie. "People are certainly a lot friendlier here than they were out west. It's weird."

"You know what else is weird?" Grant asked absently chewing on pizza. "He didn't get any pizza."

"What?" Lorie asked.

"Mr. Grease," said Grant. "He was about to go into the restaurant before, but then he left and didn't get any pizza."

"He's right," said Emily, looking up at her mom.

"Huh," said Lorie, remembering watching Griess opening the door to the pizza place but stopping when he noticed them. "Weird. Oh well, he probably just forgot. Or got a call. You know real estate agents never get to rest. The good ones are always getting calls. They have to hop-to the second they get a lead."

"I guess," said Emily, going back to picking at her salad.

When they finished lunch, the three of them decided to explore the area. Grant wanted ice cream but Emily didn't. She asked her mom if she could check out some shops alone for a few minutes.

Lorie agreed, but cautioned her not to wander too far, and she and Grant headed off up the block where they were told they'd find a handmade ice cream shop.

B. Andrew Scott

Chapter 5

Emily walked across the street towards a weird little two-story shop she'd noticed as they drove in. Nestled between a head shop and coffee roaster was a recessed store front with the name ***The Sacred Flame Books & Supplies*** painted in yellow and gold on the shop window.

Around the name were taped a number of fliers and handbills for yoga classes, meditation groups, therapeutic painting sessions, book clubs, coffee house concerts, and various social justice organization meetings.

Emily pushed on the door and a small bell tinkled overhead. The shop was dark, and her nose was instantly filled with the smells of incense and patchouli. There was strange but also kind of incredible music playing from some unseen speakers. It was like middle eastern chanting mixed with new age melodies and EDM beats.

There were three rows of tall bookshelves leading toward the back of the store. A display rack was lined with tiny bottles of essential oils. Emily twisted the top of off one with a purple label that read *Peace & Calming*. She held it to her nose and inhaled.

It was earthy and spicy and somewhat electric. She liked it. The counter was a long glass case inside of which was a selection of silver jewelry; five-pointed pentacles, ohms, and other religious symbols.

There were small ornate knives with a hand-written sign that said Athames. Along shelves behind the display case were statues of dragons, fairies, and sexy elves.

The shop's walls were lined with paintings of women, most with animals, many in flowing dresses or cloaks, some stark naked. Some were skinny. Some curvy. Some were flat out robust. But they were all beautiful. They looked like real women, even if some held fire in their hands and others had glowing eyes.

Emily's eyes fell on a painting of a dark haired woman resting on some ancient steps completely nude. One ankle rested on the other, keeping her thighs close together. She was reclining with each arm resting on the back of a large gray wolf. Each beast's tongue wagged from the side of its mouth closest to her breasts.

The woman in the picture smiled playfully while behind her, flames appeared to engulf alabaster columns.

Emily somehow knew what it was supposed to be at once. It was a twisted depiction of Romulus and Remus, alongside their mother, Rhea Silvia.

Instead of the two human twins suckling from a she-wolf, this one had turned the legend on its head. This was not depicting the birth of Rome; it was the ancient city's demise.

Like her mother, Emily had become very interested in wolf-related folklore recently. It seemed only natural. But as beautiful and well-detailed as this work was, something about the picture disturbed her.

"What are *you* doing in here?" a voice asked behind Emily.

Emily shrieked, startled. She spun around. It was that weird girl she'd seen earlier at the school. She had appeared behind the counter holding a box of red candles.

"*Jesus*," Emily exhaled. "You scared the shit out of me."

"Did you follow me?" the girl demanded.

"What?" Emily asked. "No. I just had lunch at that pink pizza place. I was checking out the town. Wait, why would I follow you anyway? Who are you?"

"Don't you know my mother?" she asked. "You're not the first to come here looking for her."

"How the heck would I know your mother?" Emily asked incredulously. "I just wanted to see what this store was all about. I didn't know you worked here."

"I don't just work here." The girl stared at her through her glasses. She set the box down. "So you didn't come to kill her?"

"Whoa," Emily said, completely lost. "Are you high? I'm not

. . . what the hell are you talking about?"

"Okay, I'm sorry," the girl said, setting the box down. She paused for a moment, almost as if resetting, and adjusted her glasses. "It's just that, people have tried. That's all. And I could tell at the school you're . . . well, I have this ability. I can sense things."

"Okay, now you're freaking me out," Emily said. Was this chick crazy? Was she psychic? Either way, Emily worried that maybe this wasn't a safe person for her to be around. She slowly started making her play for the door.

"Look," she said, casually stepping backward, "I'm sorry if I wasn't supposed to come in here. I didn't know *the rules*. I thought this was the kind of store that actually wanted customers. My bad. I'll just go."

"No, *Emily*, wait," the girl said.

Emily froze. "What the fuck? How'd you know . . ."

"Your name?" the girl said. "Sorry, it's part of my ability. I'm Morgan."

"Okay then, *Morgan*. Did you really read my mind, or did you just hear it at the school?"

"Emily Morrison from someplace called Portales," Morgan said. "You were adopted as a baby by Adam and Lorie. Your dad's a doctor. No, wait, a scientist or something."

"Okay now you're just freaking me out," Emily raised her hands. "Who the hell are you?"

"I told you," she said. "I'm Morgan. Morgan Bassett. My mom is Ella Bassett. This is her store."

"I don't give a shit about your mom or your store," said Emily. "How did you know all that stuff?"

"I'm a . . . well, *we* are witches," Morgan answered with a forced smile and a shrug, as if trying to lighten the weight of what she just said.

"Witches," Emily parroted. "Since when do witches read minds?" I thought you rode brooms and danced naked in the woods."

"That's pretty close-minded from someone like you," Morgan shot back. "I thought werewolves killed chickens and dodged silver bullets."

"You know about that too?" Emily gasped. Her eyes went wide. "What the fuck?"

"Listen, I'm a witch," she started to explain. "I could practically smell it on you."

"I thought witches made potions in big black pots," Emily said, half-hoping it stung.

"I'm not trying to upset you," said Morgan. "I'm a different kind of witch. We don't ride broomsticks. We don't dance in the woods and have orgies under the moonlight." She paused. "Well, okay, that does happen sometimes. Witches aren't embarrassed or repressed about sexuality, but it doesn't define us either. Nor should it define anyone."

"So, are you, like, pagans?" Emily asked.

"Sort of," Morgan said. "My mother and I adhere to a lot of those ideas, but we're also different. Our power is special. The way she puts it, she's more connected to the roots from which paganism and WICCA were born."

"I mean, it's probably going to sound crazy to you but, then again, you're are a werewolf. My mom is very powerful, naturally. Some witches rely on enchanted items or totems."

"You mean like magic wands?" Emily asked.

"In a way," Morgan answered, stifling an eyeroll. "Mom doesn't need that stuff. And neither do I. The power is just in us, or at least, we channel it. Basically, our bodies *are* our wands."

"Whoa," Emily gasped.

"But the older my mom gets, it seems some of her powers are diminishing," Morgan said. "She says that's normal. And strangely enough, mine are getting stronger. I don't even have to do anything. My magick is becoming instinctual. That's how I read your mind, and how I sensed what you really are."

"It's not who I *really am*," said Emily, offended.

"Sorry," said Morgan, realizing how it probably sounded. "I didn't mean it like that. But, still, you know you're something very powerful. And please don't take this wrong way, but, scary too."

"Screw you," snapped Emily, who did take it the wrong way. It seemed like the only way to take it. "You don't know me."

"Maybe not," Morgan responded, "but maybe I can help you. Look, I'm not exactly looking for a new gal pal either, but you might want to know someone with powers like mine. You're not the only *monst* . . . err, I just mean, you're not the only one with a secret on Lune de Sang."

"Monster?" said Emily, who felt anger burning her ears. She flipped Morgan the bird. "Really? You can actually go fuck yourself. You don't know anything about me, bitch. And by the way, I'm never buying anything in your stupid little store either!"

Emily stormed out of the door. The girl's words had shaken her. How the hell did this girl know her secret? Were witches psychic? Were psychics really even psychic?

A few years ago she'd have said no, that it was all phony. But now, given her own plight, she had to consider almost anything was possible.

She folded her arms across her chest and stomped off down the sidewalk to look for her mom and brother. She heard the chime of the old copper bell behind her.

"Emily, wait," Morgan called after her. "Don't go. I'm sorry. I wasn't trying to piss you off."

"Yeah, well, you did," Emily said, stopping and swinging her head around, irritated.

"I'm not very good at talking to most people," Morgan said with a sigh. "Any people, really. I don't have a lot of friends. It's pretty much my mom, and my cat. I'm such a cliché, I know."

"What about a coven?" Emily asked, somewhat sarcastically.

"*Actually, I do have a coven*," Morgan sneered. "But they're all over the place, and most of them are my mom's age. They only come to town for our meetings. There just aren't many witches like us. And I do not fit in at school, as you'll soon see."

"Is it really bad there?" Emily asked after a moment.

"Most of it," Morgan answered. "It's either preppies, hipsters, or jocks. It's like a modern John Hughes movie, and people like me, like us, are the Ally Sheedy's."

"Who?" Emily asked.

"Oh, you are kidding me," Emily rolled her eyes. "Damn it girl, I really am going to have to take care of you, aren't I?"

"What are you talking about?" Emily shrugged, hands in the air.

"I basically had a message," said Morgan. "It's a long story, and too hard to explain right now. But I feel like maybe I'm supposed to help you. Guide you, I guess, while you're here."

"Listen, I appreciate it," said Emily, hearing her brother's voice coming from somewhere nearby. She turned and saw her mom and Grant across the street. "And your apology. It's totally fine. But I don't need a guide. I've been doing okay on my own."

"Yeah, I bet," said Morgan. "But this place, and that island you live on now aren't like New Mexico. You're in a whole new world now."

"Thanks, *Jasmine*," said Emily. "I'll figure it out. I'll just, uh, . . . I'll see you in school."

"Yeah," said Morgan, watching her go. "You will."

B. Andrew Scott

Chapter 6

The following week, classes began at Bennett High School. Emily rode across the bridge with her dad, staring absently out the passenger window of his silver Prius at the green waters of the tributary flowing toward the sea.

"Are you okay, kiddo?" her dad asked, patting her arm.

"Yeah, I'm good," Emily said, slowly turning to look at him. Her dad was giving her his worried look, eyes drooping behind his glasses, accentuating the premature crow's feet. She reached out and pushed his hanging bangs behind his tortoise shell frames. "You need a haircut."

"One of these days," he smiled, looking back at the road. "It's not the top of my priority list. You are, you know? That's why we moved here. It's why I took this job."

"I know," she said softly. She hated discussing her condition. Obviously, she knew what her dad did for her every time she changed.

The risks he took to take care of her. Emily was constantly afraid she might actually hurt one of them someday, or Grant. She worried she was of placing the people she loved the most in grave danger. It was a constant weight on her heart.

"I'll figure this out," Adam Morrison assured her. "You should see this lab. I've got everything I could possibly need to help you."

"But how dad?" Emily asked. "What do you think you're going to be able to do?"

"I've told you, this condition has got to be a genetic anomaly," he said. "I just need to find the gene, and isolate it. There are people there who can help."

"People?" she repeated, looking worried. "What do you mean? You can't tell people about me."

"No, honey, I know," he said reassuring her. "They have no idea. They don't even know where the samples are from. As far as the team knows, they were sent in from an anonymous donor. They won't even know what the aberration is. How could they? Hell, I could actually tell them they're looking at cells from a werewolf. They'd just laugh at me. At least I hope they'd laugh, and not have me locked up."

He looked at her seriously, then broke into a smile.

"Look, all the other eggheads at work know is that there's something unusual with the cells. That's enough for them to go on. With extra eyes, I have a better chance at finding it, and reversing it. Or curing it. Whatever you want to call it."

"You make it sound so simple," Emily said. "I know you're a scientist, but, what if it's more like the old stories. The horror movies and stuff. Admit it, dad, somebody must've known something to write those horror novels. If I'm real, maybe the old stories were too. We just never knew it."

"What are you saying Em? he said. "That you're cursed? That you wandered off a path and got bit by a werewolf and you somehow forgot? Honey, there's no such thing as the supernatural. There's a scientific explanation. There always is."

"I hope so," she said.

"We'll get this figured out," he said. "Whatever it takes. I won't let this thing keep you from having a normal life. I promise."

"Thanks daddy," she said, looking out the window so he wouldn't see the tears in her eyes.

School was actually fine.

As fine as any other anyway. Emily kept to herself, as usual. It was like any other high school. Lots of cliques. None she really wanted to be around. She ate her first few lunches alone at the end of a table populated by the members of the marching band. They didn't seem to notice her either, which was perfectly fine.

One thing she did notice was that nobody in this school looked like her. In New Mexico most of the kids were Latino, or Native like she was, so her black hair blended right in with everybody else. This school seemed like it was 90% white kids with blonde hair, blue eyes, and perfect teeth.

And they all seemed to have adapted to the balmy, humid weather. They wore stylish clothes. It looked like a commercial shoot for Abercrombie & Fitch. Emily on the other hand wore a black tank top with her thin sweatshirt tied around her waist and shorts.

These kids smelled too. Not like sweat or anything. But the boys seemed to be having a competition to see who could douse themselves with the most cologne. Emily's sense of smell was hyper-sensitive, even in her *normal* form. The perfumed chemical odors were going to choke her to death, she was certain.

On her third day, Emily was pushing the cafeteria macaroni and cheese around her plate when a familiar hemp shoulder back plopped down on the table across from her. She looked up to see Morgan standing before her, wild hair pulled back in a white head band, wearing a black tee that read "Don't Be A Basic Witch."

"How's the first week going?" she asked.

"Um, it's going like high school," Emily answered with a shrug. She noticed Morgan had books under one arm but no tray. "Aren't you eating?"

"I never eat this food," she answered. "Nor do I eat in this cafeteria. I find the football players insufferable, even from across the room."

"So where and what do you eat?" Emily smiled at the weirdo. She wouldn't admit outload but there was something fiercely independent, or maybe just stubborn, about this girl that she couldn't stop herself from liking.

"I bring my own food," Morgan answered, "And I usually eat in the art studios downstairs. Mr. Gervais doesn't care. He usually slips out to his van to smoke a joint and take a nap."

"Cool," said Emily, raising her eyebrows. "So, I guess you're heading that way?"

"No, I already ate," Morgan answered. "Sushi. Mom and I rolled it last night. I was just grabbing some hot water for tea. You're welcome to eat there too if you'd rather. I mean, like tomorrow obviously, or whatever."

"Okay, cool," said Emily. "Uh, thanks."

"Listen, um, I don't know if you have a ride picking you up or whatever," Morgan started, "but maybe you could stop by my place after school tonight, if you want. I found something I think you'd like."

"Oh, really?" Emily asked. "Where is your *place*?"

"Duh," said Morgan, tapping herself on the forehead. "Sorry, you don't know. The store. Sacred Flame. We live upstairs. My mom and I. There's an apartment up . . . well, you get it."

"Cool, uh, yeah ," Emily chuckled at her awkwardness. Did she really want to hang out with this person? Yes, she kind of did, actually. Though she wasn't sure why. "I'll just have my dad pick me up in *Stork Circle*, or whatever it's called."

"Heron Square," Morgan laughed. "Cool. I have study hall last period so I usually just leave early and go to the shop. I'll be there when you get done."

"Cool," Emily said again. "Thanks."

But Morgan just continued to stand there, not saying anything. She was fidgeting nervously with her million bracelets.

"Don't you still need hot water?" Emily finally asked.

"Oh, yeah," said Morgan, grabbing her bag. "Sorry just, . . . yeah, hot water. Anyway, uh, come by later." She gave a half-waive and headed off.

Emily laughed and shook her head, returning to her now cold mac n cheese. She wondered what Morgan had found that she could need. That's when she noticed a couple of preppy kids at the next table watching Morgan walk away.

She heard them hissing words like "dork" and "nerd" between chuckles, and then the harsh word "dyke" which she detested. Emily dug her finger nails into the table. Then she suddenly realized she was glaring at them, and they had noticed it was well.

"What the fuck are you looking at, goth princess?" one muscular guy with closely cropped brown hair and a green American Eagle polo-style shirt snapped at her. His name was Tate Billings. They were in the same Pre-Calculus and Economics classes.

She'd also seen him pulling into the school parking lot that driving a shiny silver SUV. It was clearly brand new as it still had dealer plates. Apparently, Tate's parents had a different idea about back-to-school supplies than hers did.

Emily seemed to remember seeing the same truck parked in front of a mansion on the same street as that strange smoking girl she'd noticed her first day on the island. He obviously lived on Lune De Sang too.

Tate Billings turned back to his gaggle of baboons in Abercrombie & Fitch. "I don't get it," he said loudly. "Why do all the fucking freaks and fags keep moving here?"

"I don't know man," answered one of his buddies, a freckly ginger dressed almost identically. "Don't they know they'd be happier somewhere else?"

"Who gives a fuck what would make them happy?" Tate sneered. "I'd be happier. Ugly lezbos don't belong here."

"Yeah, just the hot ones," his buddy gurgled.

They all slapped hands and did a weird, complicated handshake like they were in a secret club.

Emily felt a familiar twitch in her temple. She was seething. Her arms began to tremble. *Uh-oh*, she thought. This never happened in the daytime, let alone when she was wide awake. Her emotions were getting the better of her.

She quickly swung her pack over her shoulder and grabbed her tray to leave. She could hear the boys laughing. *Don't listen*, she told herself. She was scared now. Not of them. Of herself. Of letting the anger take control of her.

"Don't let it loose here," a voice in her mind told her as she stood frozen for a moment, eyes shut tight. *"Just get out of here. Go."*

Emily quickly walked to the trash and dumped the rest of her lunch. As she shuffled out of the lunch room she caught sight of Morgan, still lurking in the cafeteria entrance across the room. She'd been watching the whole time.

Emily was embarrassed, but the strange witch girl gave her a gentle, if not pained smile and nodded, as if she knew what was happening in her head.

"Don't let those *cro-mags* get to you," said a black girl with round-rimmed glasses resting in her curly hair, suddenly appearing in front of Emily.

She was carrying a number of books, and a tablet. "They're typical rich, white CIS dickheads. Most of them anyway. Statistically at least a couple of them have to be secretly gay and terrified their meathead buddies will find out."

"Oh, I," Emily started. "Thanks. Yeah, I've dealt with plenty of jerks like that before."

"I'm Francesca," she said. "Frankie. Just wanted to say hi, and sorry for that. Not everyone here is like that."

"Hi, uh, I'm Emily."

"I know," Frankie laughed. "We have P.E. at the same time. I noticed you kind of hang back by the wall though."

"Yeah," said Emily, awkwardly. "Sports aren't really my thing."

"I hear you," Frankie nodded. "Me either. I'm taking a couple college courses at night. Trying to get ahead since I'm probably graduating next year. But I do like to stay active. Sometimes my brain moves faster than even I can handle. It's good to have a physical release. Anyway, if you ever need a partner, let me know. I think we start badminton next week."

"Oh, okay," said Emily, a bit overwhelmed. This girl rattled off words like machine gun fire. "Thanks."

"Of course," Frankie nodded with a smile. "Okay, gotta to run. I've got A.P. Calculus in 2 minutes."

"Oh, yeah," Emily looked at the clock. "I've got . . . Pre-Algebra."

Frankie smiled and they turned and walked in opposite directions. Emily looked for Morgan again, but she was gone.

That afternoon when school was over, Emily texted her father:

> *Hey Daddy ~ Heading to Heron Square to meet-up with a friend for a bit.*

He texted back: *You made a friend already? That's great!*

> *Relax dad, she's kind of weird.*

Emily thought for a second, and smiled.

> *But yeah, she's kind of cool too.*

Emily pushed open the door to Sacred Flame Books & Supplies to the smells of essential oils and burning sandal wood. Stevie Nicks was playing overhead. Morgan was there, setting out a display of crystals on the counter alongside a figure of tree with a face. A handwritten tag said *The Green Man.*

A fat sand colored lizard with a spiked head was sprawled out on the counter, basking in the light from an adjustable desk lamp. The creature was nearly two feet long from snout to tail. Emily was caught off guard. Reptiles were an everyday sight in New Mexico, but not usually just chilling out on countertops.

It lazily raised its head when Emily walked in and eyed her suspiciously, cocking its head sideways.

"You came," Morgan looked up, seemingly surprised, but pleased.

"I said I would, right?" Emily asked, puzzled. "Is it still cool?"

"Yes, absolutely," she answered, quickly moving around from the back of the long counter. "I just, you know. I can sometimes come off as intense, and *weird*. People sometimes humor me to make me go away. I have trouble dealing with the *mundanes* at school."

"I can understand that," said Emily. "Especially the ones like that *dick bag,* Tate. What an asshole."

"Yes, he is," Morgan nodded. "Fucker grabbed my boob last year."

"What?" Emily gasped. "Are you serious?"

"Yup," Morgan nodded. "I went to the guidance counselor

and they called him into the office, but he never got in any real trouble."

Morgan made air quotes with her fingers. "And I was told girls who are as *developed* as I am shouldn't wear tank tops."

"Are you kidding me?" Emily gasped. "That's such bullshit."

"And that was from Vice Principal Saunders," Morgan said. "So much for women looking out for women. But whatever, it's fine. I mean, it's not. But I've heard he's done much worse to other girls. And he always gets away with it. His dad's a politician or something."

"That shouldn't matter," Emily said.

"Nope, it shouldn't," Morgan shrugged. "It's against my code to bring harm to another person, except in self-defense. But goddamn if I wouldn't love to practice a few forbidden spells on his preppy ass."

"I almost lost it on him in the lunch room today," Emily said. "I mean lost it, the big bad way. Thank God I was able to calm it down."

"Umm, well, about that," Morgan smiled, squinting her eyes behind her glasses. "Maybe you didn't entirely calm yourself down. You had help."

"What do you mean, I had help?" Emily asked.

"Me," she explained. "I could hear what was going on in your brain, and I sensed it was about to get ugly."

"You were in my brain?" Emily asked, not feeling happy

about it.

"Emily, if you were to, you know, *wolf out* at school it would be Bad News Bears," Morgan explained. "I told your subconscious to stay calm and to get you the hell out of there before it revealed itself in front of the entire school and put both of you in serious danger."

"But, you were *in* my brain," Emily said again.

"Yes, and I'm sorry," she said. "I know it's a violation. But I never would have done it if I hadn't sensed serious danger. If you'd lost control, it would have been terrible. And there'd be no going back. Your whole family would be in danger."

"No, I get that," said Emily, shaking her head. "But you can't just jump into my brain. If you want to be friends or whatever this is, you're not allowed to control my mind. Call me old fashioned."

"Fair enough," said Morgan, understanding. "You're right. I didn't mean to piss you off. Like I said, the situation looked dangerous."

"It was," said Emily, embarrassed. "I'm not . . . I'm not really pissed. Just, please, don't do it again, okay? Not without asking. I mean, you know, unless it's really an emergency."

"I promise," said Morgan. She just stood behind the counter, not saying anything else. Even the lizard looked over at her expectantly.

"Who's this?" Emily asked, pointing at the reptile, intentionally changing the subject.

"Oh, that's Neil," Morgan answered, scratching him under the chin. "He's a bearded dragon."

"Wow," said Emily, with surprise. "I kind of expected any pet of yours to have a more magical name than *Neil.*

"He's named after the amazing Neil Gaiman," Morgan responded.

She scooped Neil up, who immediately looked annoyed, and snuggled him against her chin. "And he's not *mine.* We take care of each other. I just do most of the work."

"So, what did you want to show me here anyway?" Emily asked.

"Oh, right," said Morgan, letting Neil squirm out of her arms. He quickly skittered across the counter to his light, looking back at Morgan as if offended. "I'm such an idiot, I almost forgot. Check this out!"

She slipped away from behind the counter and darted down one of the dark aisles between book shelves. A second or two later she came back out holding a dusty brown leather book.

"Someone brought this in yesterday," she said, approaching Emily. "It's so random, like the Universe delivered it on purpose." Morgan spit in her hand and rubbed it across the dusty cover.

"What are you talking about?" Emily asked, shaking her head and taking the book.

Emily saw the title stamped in fading gold lettering, but she had no idea what it said. She tried, and failed, to sound it out.

"*Das Krieger . . . Das Kriegerish . . .* this is crazy. What is it, German?"

"Yes," Morgan said, excitedly. She said the title with an exaggerated German accent. "*Das Kriegerische Durst Nach Blut!*"

"Yeah, but see, about that," Emily started, lost. "I don't speak German. I didn't know you did either for that matter."

"I don't," Morgan laughed. "Well, not very much anyway. But I'm able to translate."

"Wait, how can you translate a language if you don't speak it?" Emily asked.

"I'm a witch, bitch," Morgan winked. "It's called The Warring Thirsts for, well, you can figure out *blut* can't you?"

"No," said Emily. "Blut? Wait, is it *blood*? The Warring Thirsts for Blood?"

"Yes," Morgan's eyes lit up again. "*Eine Abhandlung von Professor Gunther Beck. Universität Greifswald – 2. September 1941.* It's a study written by this German professor, Gunther Beck. He was an occult fanatic and apparently a devout Nazi shithead as well."

"Wait, what?" Emily started. "This is a Nazi book? And you thought I'd be into it?"

"Yeah!" Morgan said, then shook her head. "No! Just, listen."

She turned her attention back to the pages and read on.

"*Für die Herrlichkeit und die gesicherte globale Herrschaft von Adolf Hitler, der nationalsozialistischen Partei und allen treuen deutschen Brüdern und Schwestern.*"

"Am I supposed to know what any of that means?" Emily asked. "I'm guessing it's not saying '*death to Hitler.*'"

"Nope, pretty much the opposite," Morgan said. "For the glory and the secure global rule of Adolf Hitler, the National Socialist Party, and all loyal German brothers and sisters."

She flipped through a few more pages in the book. "But that's not what's important. Listen to this. *Die Dämonenvampire und die Wölfe führen eine ewige Fehde, die durch Hass angeheizt wird.* Damonenvampire, and Wolfe. He's talking about vampires and *werewol* . . . err, people with your condition. *Lycanthropy.*"

"You can just say werewolf," said Emily rolling her eyes. "I mean, fuck it. Let's be honest. That's the word. I might as well accept it."

"Maybe," said Morgan. "Maybe not. Listen though. *Seit Jahrhunderten waren die Wölfe die Sklaven der Dämonen. Die männlichen Wölfe wurden gemacht, um die Vampirbienenstöcke bis zum Tag zu schützen, als sie schliefen.* Male werewolves were forced to guard vampire . . . um, beehives . . . . hives I guess. *Die Weibchen und Welpen wurden als Geisel in Gefängnislagern gehalten, die von den Fledermausbeständen bewacht wurden.* Jesus."

"It mentions Jesus?" Emily said.

"No, that was me," Morgan rolled her eyes. "It's sick. The vampires would hold the female werewolves and pups hostage to force the males to protect them. *Wenn die Männchen sich weigerten zu dienen, wurden ihre Päckchen in Stücke zerrissen, Gliedmaßen von Gliedmaßen und verbrannt, während sie noch in Schreie schreien."*

"Girl, why are you are still reading me shit that I do not understand," said Emily with a sigh.

"The overall gist is Beck is explaining to Hitler that vampires and werewolves are real, and they hate each other because the vampires essentially forced the werewolves into slavery."

"Yeah, I've seen *Underworld*," Emily rolled her eyes.

"This is real, *dingus*," Morgan said sternly. "They made the male werewolves protect them during the day when they slept. The adult females had to hunt down victims for the vampires to feed on. If they refused, the vampires would kill their pups . . . err, children. They kept them all locked up in camps."

"Oh great," said Emily. "Nazi's must've loved vampires then. They thought alike."

"No, it looks like even the Nazis were afraid of vampires," said Morgan. She slid her finger across the words on the page and for a few seconds they appeared as English.

"The vampire can never be tamed or controlled, because it is a demon. However, if it were possible to harness the power of the animal man - the wolf – which is the sworn enemy of the blut demon, the Reich would be invincible against all men."

"What the shit?" Emily asked, eyes wide, her gum dangling

out of her mouth. "Hitler wanted to use werewolves as part of his army?"

"Hitler was all about trying to use the supernatural to his advantage," Morgan nodded. "Didn't you see *Hell* . . . never mind." She flipped a couple pages further.

"Oh here," she read on. "*Sollten die Vampire diesen Plan entdecken, werden sie sich mit den Feinden Deutschlands befreien, um sich zu schützen. Sie werden es dem Führer nie erlauben, die Wölfe für seine eigene Macht zu nutzen.*

"He's saying if the vampires find out the Nazis want to use werewolves, they'll freak out. They'll probably even agree to help America. Well, he just says the enemies of Germany, but that's basically us and Britain, and Russia." Morgan scanned down the page with her finger.

"Umm, let's see, *deshalb muss unser Plan zweifach sein, um siegreich zu sein. Kontrolliere die Wölfe. Zerstöre die Vampire. Und so werden wir das Vertrauen der Wölfe gewinnen, um dem Reich zu dienen, nicht als Sklaven, sondern als Soldaten.*"

"Basically he was proposing a two-pronged plan," Morgan explained. "I read ahead a little. The Nazis wanted to form a small army of vampire hunters and werewolves, who would in turn, he hoped, show Hitler their loyalty. Then the Reich would use them as *soldaten*. Oh, I mean, uh, ..."

"Soldiers," Emily interjected, getting the idea.

"You got it," said Morgan. She held the book out toward Emily. "Here, I enchanted it for you."

"You enchanted it?" Emily said, taking the book.

"Yes, hold out your finger."

Confused, Emily pointed her finger at Morgan. The young witch grabbed her wrist and pressed her finger against the book.

"Okay," she said. "You can do the same thing with your finger now. The book will recognize you."

"Come on," Emily laughed, staring at her finger.

"Okay, do we really need to have the *magick is real* talk?" Morgan glared. "Have a little faith, Miss Full Moon Fever."

"Fair enough, you're right," Emily said, nodding. She opened the front cover and there was an inscription. "*Unus est magister in sempiternum. Unum servum sempiternum.* That's not German, is it?"

"No, sounds like Latin," said Morgan. "Go ahead. Try to translate."

Emily slid her finger over the first line the way she watched Morgan do it. "*Unus est . . . magister in . . . sempiternum.*"

After a second, the words began to change. Emily could read them easily. "One forever a master," she read loud. "*Unum servum sempiternum.*"

"One forever a slave," said a soft voice behind her, appearing from out of the bookshelves.

Startled, Emily turned and saw a middle-aged woman appear. She was beautiful, and curvy, with hair that was a combination of blonde and black streaks. She wore a loose billowing top and long muslin skirt.

Like Morgan, her wrists jingled with dozens of bracelets. She also wore a black leather string around her neck with a murky red stone at the end, encased in a silver pentacle, that rested in her ample cleavage.

"Err, Emily, this is my mom," said Morgan.

"Hello Emily," she spoke, taking Emily gently by the hand. "My name is Ella. I've heard so much about you. It's so nice to meet you in person dear. I sense your confusion and conflict, but know that you will always be welcomed and protected in this shop. No child will live in bondage to demons while I draw breath."

"Oh, um, thanks?" was all Emily could think to say.

B. Andrew Scott

Chapter 7

Later that night, while most of Lune de Sang was preparing for bed, Sophie Broussard was feeling that all too common, often all too deadly combination of boredom and restlessness that vexed her so many nights.

She'd been pacing her vast antebellum mansion looking for something to keep her mind occupied. She'd changed her outfit three times just to pass the time. For the moment, she'd settled on a short knit dress with long loose sleeves and a dark floral patterns of oranges and browns.

She finally poured herself a tall glass of Kentucky bourbon and flopped down on a white sofa in a seldom used parlor just off the entryway.

She glanced around the room at a number of paintings hung on the walls. They were all originals. All valuable. A Gustav Klimt. A Dali. One by Henri Matisse featuring naked women in the woods. Sophie often forgot they were even there. Her favorite was of a red haired singer and dancer named

Marcelle Lender, painted by Toulouse Lautrec.

Lautrec was a French artist who famously painted and lived among the seedy nightlife of the Moulin Rouge. He preferred to company of prostitutes and drunkards, and famously painted posters for the Moulin Rouge.

Sophie felt they would've been friends. And they could have been. Sophie was technically older than Lautrec, but he had been born, lived, and died while she was underground.

"Luther," Sophie finally called out, as even her paintings weren't helping to occupy her thoughts.

In a minute, her brick shithouse of an attaché appeared in the hallway. His thick shoulders testing the limits of the stitching in his white dress shirt.

"What?" he responded, tersely.

"I need ice," she said. "And I'm bored as fuck."

"You're such a lady," he grunted, turning for the kitchen.

He returned shortly with a silver bucket of ice and a matching set of tongs. His boss held up her glass and he dutifully deposited four ice cubes into her tumbler, careful not to cause a splash. "You good?"

"I'd be lost without you big guy," she winked, taking a sip.

"You're lost either way," he said. "Why don't you try to act like a responsible member of society. You came here to blend in. Go out. Try blending."

"I can't," she sighed. "You know that. Look at the people on this island. They don't want me here. They all smile and act like proper gentile citizens of the new south, but secretly they still see me as one thing first, and we both know it isn't rich. I'm still the only black girl on this island not making a bed or cooking somebody else's dinner. These people resent me, and I despise them."

"Then leave," Luther suggested. "There are a million places to go. You said you wanted to see Trinidad again. Let's go. I can arrange a private ship before the week is over."

"Oh Luther," she said, "I did love Trinidad. I felt a real connection there. Sometimes I wonder if some of my ancestors came from there. But I can't go back. Not after the last time. Have you forgotten the church mob with the machetes and torches chasing us all the way to the airstrip?"

"After your little feeding frenzy, you mean," Luther added.

"I had too much to drink," she said. "I lost control. I killed a handful of tourists climbing the hundred steps."

"A handful?" Luther choked. "Seventeen. It was seventeen Sophie, in roughly four minutes. The surf was literally running red."

"And they probably haven't forgotten," she shrugged. "The point is, I'm thinking it's a hard pass on Trini. At least for now."

"That was 1996," Luther waved her off. He picked up the decanter of bourbon and took a swig right from the crystal.

"And you were in your blonde wig phase," he added. "Even if

any witnesses are still around, none of them will remember you. As long as you keep your fangs sheathed this time. And stay away from that rum distillery."

"I don't know," said Sophie, swinging her bare feet around to the floor. She stood up and crossed toward the window. "I just feel so restless. In fact, to be honest with you, I think I feel . . . anxious. And that's not a feeling I'm used to. Something has changed on this island. I don't feel *comfortable*."

"You feel uncomfortable?" said Luther, eyebrows raised behind his glasses. He lifted the decanter. "You're about to get yourself cut off. That's good bourbon and you're swilling it like Boone's Farm at a Florida frat party. What in the hell could make Sophie Broussard feel anxious?"

"I'm serious Luther," she said. "I came back to this island to lay low. It was a safe place. Admit it, I've been very well-behaved since we got here. I haven't fed in the wild once in years."

"Only because I made that deal with our friend at the jail," Luther said, peering at her from over his dark glasses. "Is that what this is about? Is the hunger back? The pantry is empty. I could take a drive across the bridge, but, you might have to settle for something off the street."

"No, no," she said. "I mean, well, maybe. It's just, this island is my home. Shouldn't I feel comfortable here? Lately I feel like there's something strange here. Something *other*."

"Other," Luther repeated. "You mean like you?"

"No, that's just it," said Sophie. "It's something else. Something different. But powerful. And, evil."

"Said the vampire," Luther muttered.

"I am what I am," she said. "But I'm not evil. Not necessarily. I'm trying to control it, which is why you have a job, remember? I never wanted to hurt anyone. Not anyone that doesn't deserve it anyway. But this isn't about blood."

"Well I'm not sure what I can do for you," said Luther. "I haven't seen anyone unusual on this island. Nothing that would raise any red flags for me anyway, and I've developed a pretty good instinct for trouble. I've had to after spending all these years with you."

"Very funny," said Sophie, frustrated. "Maybe it's all in my head."

She stepped out onto the front porch in the night air. She didn't bother to turn on the lights. After all, she didn't need them. "I just know something's off."

Sophie stood in the dark, feeling the breeze cut through the humidity in the air. The moon was bright and silvery shining down on the ocean just across the street. Sophie listened the surf rolling in, splashing against the shore. The palmettos rustled in the wind.

These were the sounds that so many mortals lived to hear. They called it paradise. Sophie had learned to understand. The sounds of the sea were calming. It was like the leaves were talking.

These were moments when having heightened senses was a blessing. Sophie felt like she was connected to sand and the air and the water. An elusive sense of peace began to melt over her spirit again, for the first time in so long.

It wasn't easy being as old as she was, and to have such a large chunk of her memory completely missing. But she'd come to terms with it, as best she could.

The trade-off was somehow she had this amazing house, a stone's throw from sand and surf. Sure she had to stay inside most days, and cover up like a shepherd if she dared venture into the sun, but still, there were worse places. Imagine living the next century in Wisconsin.

She should stop being stupid, Sophie told herself. Sure she was a vampire, but she had a hold on it. Why shouldn't she try to have a normal life and enjoy the perks of her condition? She closed her eyes and took a deep breath, feeling the anxiety slowly clear away.

Then, as quickly as serenity came, it was disrupted, and sent scurrying away like a rabbit into the night.

"*Stupid fucking dog,*" someone was ranting, stomping down the sidewalk, dragging a Yorkshire Terrier on a leash. "Why do I always have to walk your useless ass? You aren't even mine. I wanted a real dog. A Pitt, or a Doberman or something bad ass. Not some stupid yippy rat."

It was the son of one of her neighbors. Tate, she thought his name was. Brown flat top, preppy shirt with the collar turned up. He was busy scrolling through his smart phone as he cursed the dog and his own mother's name.

This was no southern gentleman. He paused long enough to yank hard on the leash of the poor little Yorkie, nearly snapping its neck. The dog gave a tortured yelp. It was a miracle he hadn't broken it.

Sophie could feel blood filling her eyes. Sure she was no fan of little toy mutts like that either, but she couldn't stand animal abuse. And this kid was an asshole. Her gums began to swell and she could feel her teeth beginning to shift inside her mouth.

The teen happened to look up as he passed her porch and caught her staring. He sneered at her and whipped at the leash.

"Come on idiot," he barked over his shoulder, picking up his pace. Under his breath he mumbled "What are you looking at anyway, fucking half-breed."

His racial assault continued as he hurried away from the house, unaware that his target happened to have supernatural hearing far more sensitive than that of any normal human.

"Guess it's true her great-great-granddaddy liked dipping into the slave quarters in the middle of the night."

"Luther," Sophie called back into the house after a few moments. A sardonic grin had spread its wings across her face. "Don't bother driving into Charleston tonight. I'm making other plans."

"Other plans?" he asked, appearing in the doorway. "I don't

like the sound of that. You sure?"

"Of course," a mischievous grin spread across her lips. "You were right. I need to go out and get closer to the people on this island."

Chapter 8

Tate Billings was the oldest son of State Senator Charlie Billings, who was rarely ever at home, and a socialite mother Samantha Jane Montgomery-Billings, who was rarely ever sober.

His family's South Carolina roots could be traced all the way back to John Rutledge, 31st Governor of the State, and 2nd Supreme Court justice appointed by George Washington himself.

Around 1:15 in the morning, Tate's phone *dinged*, notifying him of a text. Feeling as though he'd been shaken awake from a deep sleep, he groggily reached up and grabbed the phone off his desk. What he saw made him quickly sit up and rub his eyes.

It was a pair of small but pert naked breasts with silky locks of blonde hair draped around them.

"Who the hell?" Tate whispered.

He tried enlarging the pic, desperate to catch any facial details, but no luck. He literally slapped himself in the head to think of who had long blonde hair that might be sexting him.

Brittany, he wondered, thinking of a girl in his U.S. History class? But nah, couldn't be. She seemed like a major prude. After all, he'd flirted with her a couple times and she'd frozen him out. Probably a religious bitch, he shrugged. But then, who?

A message appeared below the image.

> *You awake?*

"I am now," he whispered as he typed. He didn't want to ask who it was, for fear of pissing her off.

> *Want to sneak out and meet me? I'm house sitting for my parents' friends. We can go swimming. Naked.*

Damn, he thought, shaking his head. He may not have known who it was, but he wasn't going to turn down the opportunity to get laid in a pool.

"Definitely," he whispered as he typed. "Give me the address."

Tate hopped out of bed and threw on a tank top and quickly slipped into his bathroom to piss. He slid on nylon basketball shorts he wore around the house – he figured there was no sense in putting on underwear. He liked how the smooth material felt against his junk. Since he was about use that junk, these would help him prepare, his *bro-brain* reasoned.

Tate sprayed body spray on his chest and armpits, and nodded to his reflection in the mirror. As he was about to leave, it occurred to him that he should check his breath in a cupped hand.

Shit, he thought, smelling his foul mouth. Did he need to brush his teeth? He opted to skip proper dental hygiene in favor of shoving a few sticks of gum into his mouth.

At the end of the hall he could see the light of his mom's tv, meaning she'd fallen asleep with it on, as usual. She wouldn't hear anything.

Tate softly crept down the winding stair case to the main entry and snuck out the side door near the laundry room. The address was on the other side of the island, on Delisle Street, but it wasn't that far.

He could make the jog in ten minutes easy.

There was a thick low lying fog hovering over the wet grass. Tate stayed on the sidewalk for fear of getting his new Jordans wet. There was nobody out on the streets at this time anyway. No one would see him. And so what if they did, he thought as he rubbed his hands together? He was about to get lucky with a *freaky ass honey*.

Tate reached the address he'd been sent which was a two-story white affair at the end of a cull de sac with no fencing around the front yard, thankfully. It did however have a tall privacy fence guarding the back.

Tate walked softly up the stone walkway to the front door, but all the windows were dark. She must be in the back already. Probably kept the lights off so no snoopy neighbors would call the cops. Smart chick, he thought.

Tate slipped around the side of the house. When he reached the arched fence door, he could hear gentle splashing on the other side. He began to get excited, and nervous. His stomach was doing backflips. He couldn't believe this was really happening. It was like the plot to a porno.

It didn't even matter who was on the other side of that gate now, he thought. He was so aroused, he worried he might not last very long. What if whoever it was made fun of him, or spread it around the school that he was a two-pump chump?

To hell with that, he thought, steeling his courage. Tate grabbed the black gate handle and pressed his thumb down on the release. It opened toward him.

He stepped into the backyard, which was composed of a concrete patio with black iron furniture. Tall thick hedges lined the inside of the fence all around the yard. There was a brick barbecue blocking his view of the pool. It was too dark to see much else anyway, other than the blueish green glow of the underwater lights in the long kidney shaped inground.

The pool was clearly heated as steam rose off the water in the cooled night air. The back of the house was completely dark. Not a single sliver of light in any of the many windows.

"You made it," a girl's voice said with a playful giggle. "I wasn't sure if you would come. Close the gate, okay?"

"Oh, yeah," Tate stammered, squinting to see who it was without much luck. He could barely make out the form of a girl, shrouded by steam. She was on the far side of the pool, sitting on the edge with her legs dangling in the water. He turned back and softly closed the gate until it clicked. "My bad."

"Come over here," she said.

Tate crossed around the barbecue and stepped closer to the pool. He strained to see but still couldn't make out her face. Just a barely-there shiny bikini on was clearly a think, shapely body and her long blonde hair, just as he'd seen in the text.

"Do you remember me?" she giggled some more, swirling her feet below the surface.

"I, uh, I mean," he started. Truthfully, he couldn't tell. He was having a really hard time making out her face in the darkness. It literally felt like there was a fog in front of her face, or maybe it was in front of his. His eyes just couldn't break the opaque haze preventing him from getting a closer look at her. Tate took a step closer.

"You don't, do you?" she asked. "I can't believe you forgot. We met at Toby's birthday party in June."

"Oh," Tate responded, still clueless. He tried to jog his memory. He remembered Toby's party, at least most of it. But he had gotten pretty smashed. Toby's stepdad had bought them three kegs plus all those Fireball shots. Had he really met this hot chick and completely forget?

"I can't believe you don't remember," she said, with mock offence, but then giggling again. "Well, we were all pretty trashed. I guess I can forgive you. It has been a minute."

"Yeah, most definitely," was all Tate could say. He thought for a second. "Did we, uh, you know?"

"Hook up?" she asked with a laugh. "No, not all the way. It was fun though. I'd say we have unfinished business to take care of. I mean, if you want to, that is."

"Hell yeah, girl," he blurted out. Tate began kicking off his shoes. He pulled off his tank top and began moving aggressively around the pool, feeling himself growing even more aroused.

"Ooh, now someone's excited," she giggled.

Tate couldn't believe this was happening. He usually had to work a lot harder than this – be more forceful. This chick wanted it bad, he thought, so impressed with himself.

Still, even within a few feet of her, sitting on the edge of the pool, he couldn't see her face.

"There is something I want to do to you," she said playfully. "If it's okay."

"You can do anything you want to me," Tate answered, his voice cracking.

"Anything?" she repeated with a caution. "Be careful what you say to me."

"I'm a big boy," he said, with a dopey smile. He felt like he was about to finish in his basketball shorts from all this excitement. "But I have to admit something. I can't remember your name. What is it again?"

Her head snapped around to look right at him, her blonde hair suddenly disappeared, melting away to reveal black and amber curls. The pasty white skin he'd seen in the texted pic had turned to a rich café au lait.

The unnatural fog that seemed to be obscuring her face dissipated. The mystery girl's visage became perfectly clear, but it was not what he was hoping for.

Her forehead furrowed in a menacing scowl. Her eyes burned bright red and she opened her mouth with a hiss revealing a row of sharp white fangs.

"Justice," Sophie hissed. She leapt straight up into the air and landed on her feet just inches away from him. Veins were pulsing in her temples. "For every young girl you've ever hurt and abused, my name is *justice!*"

"Jesus," he yelled, tripping backward and scraping his heel on the concrete. "What the fuck are you? Leave me alone!"

"Now tell me about my great granddaddy," she said, savoring the scent of his fear. The silver bikini was gone. Sophie Broussard stood before him in skintight black leggings and a leather corset.

He was suddenly so scared, he involuntarily pissed himself. Sophie could smell the hot urine even before it ran out of his shorts and down his leg.

"Please," he begged. "I'm sorry. I'm an asshole. I didn't mean anything."

"No motherfucker," Sophie said, "you don't mean anything.

And nobody's going to miss you. Not even your mama."

She leapt to strike, ready to fall upon him and sink her teeth into his jugular vein, something completely unplanned happened.

A black blur came flying over the fence and in a split second, had knocked Sophie sideways, out of the air, and tackled Tate, twisting his body around like a pretzel as they both landed on the grass.

Before Sophie could shake her head and figure out what had hit her, its bone snapping jaws had clamped down on Tate's neck. It's strong, hairy black legs had wrapped around his torso, digging toe claws into his flesh. It attacked like an apex predator, immediately, savagely, incapacitating its prey.

It's sharp teeth tore deeper into the boy's thick neck, just below the chin. And with a wet, ripping sound, it tore out his throat, spraying blood into the air. Red droplets soaked into the white concrete across the patio, and spread like tiny crimson clouds in the pool.

"Are you fucking kidding me?" Sophie screamed, scrambling to her feet. "I knew it!"

The creature's head snapped back at her. It was female - a muscular female frame, covered in fine black hair from head to toe. Her hands ended in stubby padded fingers with crescent claws she was currently using to tear into Tate's chest.

Her mouth and nose had morphed into one fluid muzzle, lined with flesh-ripping teeth, including hyper extended canines along the top and bottom.

Emily's eyes had turned from brown to glowing amber, with black slits for pupils. What flesh of her face was still visible was now smeared with wet, sticky blood.

Regardless of this wolfen abomination now feeding on the writhing gurgling body of Tate Billings, Sophie Broussard immediately recognized the creature as the same girl she'd seen in the car only days before. It made perfect sense. She couldn't believe she didn't figure it out that night.

She'd felt it all the way down her spine. This must be that new evil she'd sensed on the island. And yet, it didn't feel the same. Either way, this bitch was eating her late-night snack.

"*He was mine*," Sophie yelled, leaping some 15 feet into the air, over the monster, and down on the eave hanging over the patio door.

The wolf creature watched this strange human fly through the night air and perch above her. She made a half-hearted growl, almost more a grunt, as a warning to stay away, then returned to her kill.

For Tate Billings was definitely dead now. Sure there was technically some life in him. Sophie could sense his heart still trying to pump blood in vain, but it was over. Tate had at best a few more seconds of gagging and gurgling as he desperately tried to draw in oxygen, thwarted by the gaping hole in his neck.

Tate was far past feeling the unimaginable pain that came with having one's body torn apart by a rabid monster. By now he was probably only registering unusual pressure and discomfort as his ribcage was wrenched open to a symphony of cracking bone and tearing sinew.

And as the darkness finally seeped in from the corners of his eyes, his fading brain probably tried to compute the painful, tugging sensation as this hairy demon with green eyes and pointed ears rising from a mess of black hair used its teeth to remove one of his lungs.

"Did you come for me?" Sophie demanded, her nails digging into the shingles.

But the beast ignored her, just feeding on Tate's organs.

Now Sophie was really pissed. She launched herself like a bullet, barreling into the monster. They tumbled across the hard concrete and stopped just before the pool's edge.

The beast bellowed and snapped its jaws at her. Sophie wrapped a hand around its hairy throat and bared her own fangs as if about to strike.

"Bitch, I'm talking to you!"

Sophie locked eyes with the werewolf. Somewhere in those hideously perverted features was that raven haired girl she'd seen in a minivan. Sophie's every instinct should have screamed to kill her. These things hated vampires.

And werewolves were the only creatures with the power to kill them. Even Sophie knew that.

They were ancient enemies, even if this new girl was ignorant of that long blood feud. It was probably imprinted somewhere within their tortured psyches.

And Sophie couldn't entirely blame them. Her kind had used and abused werewolves throughout history.

And yet, this wolf seemed to have little interest in killing her at all. It was as if Sophie's presence was completely irrelevant to her. Until she had attacked, that was.

This she-wolf was just out hunting. She must have been out on the prowl and smelled the rise in his blood pressure. And now she had her kill, so Sophie didn't matter.

Regardless, Sophie knew it was dangerous having a werewolf on her island – even if she was not a direct threat. Tate's would be the first of many bodies to start popping-up, looking like they'd been run through a garbage disposal.

That would bring a lot of unwanted attention to their rather private community. Police, television crews, even people who just got off on crime scenes and blood. These days there were many of those. That put Sophie at risk for unwanted exposure as well.

And yet, Sophie felt her temper cooling. Watching this poor tortured soul whose furry throat was now in her hand, she no longer had the urge to kill her. After all, wasn't this girl's condition so much worse a cross to bear. No control. No immortality. And look what it did to her skin and hair.

Sophie's grip loosened just a bit, but that was enough. With a growl the wolf seized the opportunity and, as if merely throwing off a sack of flour, tossed Sophie across the patio and crashing into the barbecue, reducing it to a pile of bricks.

In a second, Sophie was on her feet, teeth and claws fully bared.

"Well that's definitely going to wake the neighbors," Sophie spat her own blood into the rubble. "I was going to let you go. Do you really want to do this?"

The she-wolf lunged forward, snarling, but then stopped, as if dazed. Her head swiveled as her eyes rolled back in her skull, and she fell to the ground in a heap of black hair. Her body began to convulse.

Sophie witnessed the transformation as her animal snout recessed back into her skull and her face once again appeared human. The black hair that covered her body retracted deep into her pores until she was again pale and pink, save for the long straight human hair on her head.

Transfixed, Sophie knelt over Emilie's body and pushed the sweaty, matted black hair out of her face. She imagined herself as a teenager – a true teenager – what little of it she could remember. What would her life have become, had she only been a normal girl?

Sure, life at that time in history would have at times been difficult for a child of mixed heritage to say the least. There were safe places she could have gone. Safe havens where no one would have called her the child of the devil himself. She might have been able to have a family, and even grow old, and dying as was the natural way of things, surrounded people who loved her.

Would this girl ever have that chance, or would she too live a haunted life of solitude, always looking over her shoulder for a stake, or in her case, a silver bullet? Would she constantly wrestle with the horror of the things she had to do to survive?

"You poor beautiful thing," Sophie whispered, feeling a swell of pity for the child. "Who did this to you?"

"Get away from her," a man's voice demanded.

Sophie whirled around, alarmed. Her eyes blazed red and the confusion on her face gave way to a terror-inducing scowl as her vein-piercing fangs emerged.

A man in a dark jogging suit with wild blonde bed head was standing in the open gateway pointing a pistol at her. She saw his eyes widen in surprise. She instantly smelled his fear.

And that's when he panicked and squeezed the trigger and something hard bounced off Sophie's skull. Followed by two more slugs. The impact made her head spin and she clumsily fell into the water like a drunken diver.

"It's okay baby," Adam Morrison said, running to his daughter's side. He knelt beside her and began to wrap her in a blanket.

"Daddy's right here," he tried to comfort her as always. Inside his heart was pounding like the first night he'd discovered what his daughter was. He shouldn't have killed that woman, he thought.

Whoever she was, or *whatever*, he shouldn't have lost

control. But it didn't matter now. Only Emily mattered. "It's going to be okay. Let's get you home."

The surface of the pool erupted like a depth charge had been detonated. Sophie burst straight up out of the water with a demonic scream and launched herself at the frightened man.

She grabbed him by the collar as she landed and her wet feet slid across the grass, dragging him behind her.

"Wrong night to play hero, big boy," Sophie growled, her ruby eyes smoldering. She lifted him off the ground with one hand. "I came out to hunt tonight, damn it, and I'm sick of being interrupted!"

"Please," Adam begged. "I was protecting my daughter. I just want to get her out of here."

"Your what?" Sophie asked, her eyes immediately dimming. She looked at the unconscious girl and then back at him. She loosened her grip and let him drop. "Damn it!"

At that moment, Morgan Basset, who had ridden her bicycle to Emily's house to bring her something and saw Dr. Morrison leaving and followed him, bust through the open on a Schwinn cruiser with a basket on the handle bars, wearing flannel *Gryffindor* pajama bottoms and a hooded sweatshirt.

Morgan had seen the van outside the dark house and the man walking around to the backyard with a gun. As soon as she came through the gate and saw Emily lying on the ground, and the vampire holding her dad in the air, Morgan reacted without hesitation.

She'd begun committing a specific spell to memory the day she had learned that Sophie Broussard, the heir of Monsieur Levasseur, bloodthirsty founder of Lune de Sang, was haunting her ancestral home.

"Bana-diaid a h-uile duine, cuir cumhachd na grèine gu do nighean airson a bhith a 'bualadh air an diabhal," Morgan cried out, both hands in the air before her, fingers twisting as if knitting invisible threads. *"Bhris solas air ais an diabhal. Air ais dhan dorchadas a bheil i ann an trom ghaol!"*

Blinding white light suddenly filled the fenced in yard, so bright even Adam's eyes burned until he shielded them with his arm. For Sophie, it was utter agony.

While unlike in fictional tales, Sophie would not burst into flame when exposed to direct sunlight, it did hurt like hell. It made her light sensitive eyes feel as though they were about to explode, and seared her skin like a bacon on a flat-top grill in a greasy diner. In other words, it really sucked.

"Bhris solas air ais an diabhal. Air ais dhan dorchadas a bheil i ann an trom ghaol!" Morgan called out again, even louder.

"Fuck," Sophie roared, clawing at her eyes. "Enough already. I give up."

Clearly this night was not going to end up in her favor. Sophie decided she should've listened to Luther. She leapt all the way over the pool to the back fence where she balanced like a cat on the narrow edge of the boards.

She cast one last hiss at Morgan, eyes squinted tight as she was engulfed in a deluge of ultraviolet rays, then leapt off into the trees on the other side. In a moment, she was gone.

Adam scrambled back over to his daughter, cradling her in his arms. He looked up at Morgan, tears in streaming down his face. He nodded to her in gratitude, unable to speak.

"Is she okay?" Morgan asked.

"Yes," he said breathlessly. Adrenaline was still surging through his body. "As okay as she can be. This is how it goes."

"This happens every time?" Morgan asked, helping him to lift her up.

"Yes," said Adam. "I'm sorry, you're Morgan, aren't you?"

"Sorry, yeah, hi," Morgan answered. "I was with Emily earlier today at the bookstore."

"Right, she told me," he said. "I've seen you and your mom a couple times. That's your family's bookstore, huh? Now I guess it makes more sense. I mean, none of it really does, but still. Did you know him?"

He nodded to the mangled remains of a teenager a few feet away.

"Tate?" she asked, looking back at the mess on the ground. There was blood everywhere, staining the patio and glistening in the grass.

Tate's body was no longer human. It was a horror movie prop. His remaining entrails were strewn across the concrete.

"Yes. I did. And if it helps, he wasn't a good person. Not that I wish a horrific death on anyone, but, if it had to happen, he was probably a deserving target."

"He was young," Adam offered. "People can change."

"Not on Lune de Sang," said Morgan. "Not people like Tate."

"She can't control it," Adam said, more to himself for the ten-thousandth time.

"I know," said Morgan, putting a gentle hand on his shoulder.

"Thank you, by the way, for showing up when you did."

"I'm just glad I made it," she said following him to the van. "Sophie is dangerous. I had a feeling if she ever discovered what Emily is, she'd come for her."

"Sophie would be the vampire with the glowing eyes and long fangs?" he said, huffing as he carried Emily to the van. "Good God, my life just keeps getting stranger."

"Sophie Broussard," Morgan said. "She own the big house on Saint Charles. She's the ancestor of a famous southern vampire, but no one seems to realize it. She's got the whole island under some kind of trance."

"That's a neat trick," Adam rolled his eyes, sliding the van door shut.

"This is the first time I've ever caught her out to feed," Morgan said. "My mom says she's got a familiar who brings her bodies to keep her out of sight. I worried Emily's arrival might throw things out of whack. Sophie probably sensed her as soon as you all moved in."

"What does that mean?" Adam asked. "That thing wants to kill Emily?"

"I don't know," she answered. "Vampires and werewolves have a long history of bad blood. The good news is Emily will be fine by day. We'll just have to take precautions at night."

"That can be a challenge with Emily's condition," he said. "Thank you again Morgan. Do you need a ride home or something?"

"No, I have my bike," she answered, staring past him at the sleeping girl on the seat inside the car. "I'm good. Just, you know, take care of her. Ask her to text me if she doesn't come to school tomorrow."

"Yes, of course," he said, crossing around the van and getting into the driver's seat. "I owe you one Morgan. You saved both of our skins."

"I'm a witch," Morgan smiled with a mock salute, "that's my job."

The van turned around in the cul-de-sac and drove slowly down the heavily wooded street with the lights off.

Morgan walked back to where she'd left her bike and rode down the sidewalk toward the other side of the island and across the Sayle Bridge back to Charleston.

Meanwhile back at 307 Delisle Street, Tate Billings lay dead and disemboweled in the eerie glow of the swimming pool lights. The patio door slid open quietly and a man stepped out of the dark house.

He wore a black button-down shirt, tan pants, and expensive designer shoes. In one hand he clutched a black velvet bag.

Amman Griess assessed the carnage on the patio before him and sighed. This wasn't entirely what he'd hoped for. He turned back and looked at his reflection in the patio door and started smoothing back his shiny black hair as he considered what to do next.

He stopped when he noticed a strange spot. The skin where his neck met his jaw had begun to tighten and discolor. He probed it with his finger and a small portion of the flesh tore away, revealing drying fibrous muscle and exposed jawbone.

"Damn it," he whispered. Griess walked over to the remains of Tate Billings and bent down, digging two fingers in the soft, gooey innards of his mutilated torso.

He began to rub the boy's sticky blood on the spot along his jawbone, working it into the wound. The muscle began to soften and regenerate, and new flesh grew over the hole.

"That's better," he said.

Griess reached into the velvet bag and removed a strange item of gold. The bottom ended in a sharp sickle-like blade, and the top had been molded into an ancient ankh – the Egyptian symbol for life. It was similar to a Christian cross but with a loop at the top like the eye of the needle.

This sacred relic, and the symbol after which it had been fashioned, predated Christianity by thousands of years. Inside this one's circle was an ornately crafted eye - the Eye of Horus. This was an ancient and enchanted artifact. Griess held it up.

"Hear me and come forth damned souls," Griess said in the forgotten tongue of an ancient people. "Take the wretched remains of this oafish mortal from my sight. He served his purpose. Now drag him below to be forgotten."

The ground around Tate's body began to tremble and quake and the concrete of the patio was transformed to sand.

Decrepit, rotted hands began to dig their way up through the ground beneath his body and claw at his stiffening limbs.

Sulfurous yellow smoke rose from the earth as the mutilated body of Tate Billings was pulled down into the sand, and after a few moments he was completely gone. The sand once again hardened into concrete.

"Now, cleanse this place," Griess spoke again, waiving the ankh through air. The water in the swimming pool began to ripple and churn until it made a whirlpool circling around the perimeter of the four pool walls.

A rotating pillar of water rose from the pool and then collapsed over the blood stained patio and lawn, washing away every trace of the attack that had occurred there. The water then flowed, as if alive, back into the pool.

"Good enough," said Griess.

He walked around the house to the front yard and noticed something was missing. Annoyed, Griess looked around, and saw it under a large hedge. He retrieved the heavy post with the tin sign and placed it back to a hole dug in the yard. Once again, his smiling face hung in the front yard alongside the words: **FOR SALE**.

Griess pulled his Mercedes out of the garage and down the driveway. He had other business to attend to. This night hadn't gone as he had hoped. No matter, he thought. The two beasts were now aware of one another, and a battle to the death was inevitable.

Neither could allow the other to live much longer. That was how they were fated. He would just have to do all he could to ensure the wolf won.

What he hadn't anticipated was the young sorceress. How could he have been so foolish? He'd seen that shop in town so many times.

He'd just assumed they were charlatans and nothing to worry about. True witches were so rare in this millennium.

Still, Amman thought, absently fingering at the newly healed spot on his jawline, she might prove to be an asset. She had been aiding the wolf against the blood demon. And the enemy of my enemy, as they said.

It was astounding, Amman thought. Who knew the new world would be so fraught with evil creatures. In his day, such devils were contained to the underworld. It only served to further bolster his resolve. Without the supreme rule of his people, all manner of demons had been allowed to run amok. They would leave the planet in ruins.

This must be the reason the gods had allowed him to be killed in one life, so that he might rise again in this one. It wasn't cruelty. It was destiny.

Griess gripped the steering wheel tighter, pressed harder on the accelerator, and squealed his tires as he rounded a corner. Now he would right all wrongs created in this unchecked world, as *Ra* commanded.

And in return, he would rule over humanity as a god on Earth.

Chapter 9

The next morning Emily woke up clean and dressed in fresh pajamas, as she always did after an episode. Her memories were still little more than shards of a broken stained glass window - a piece here, another there - but it did seem like she was able to recall a bit more than usual.

A particularly disturbing image was that of a young man with blood spattered all over his face. It looked very much like the loudmouthed bully Tate from the cafeteria the day before.

Emily shuffled down the hall, into the kitchen where her mom was pouring cereal for Grant who was seated at the counter, cackling at videos of other spastic kids on his tablet. Her dad was sitting at the small table, staring absently out the patio door over a cup of coffee. He looked tired.

The small tv mounted over the pantry had the morning news playing.

> *"Officials from the U.S. Treasury Department*
> *are refusing to comment on whether they have*

any suspects or exactly how much gold the truck was carrying," the overly-made up blonde anchor was saying. *"Sources say a truck this size traveling between Fort Knox and the New York Depository could easily be carrying $20 to $25 million dollars in gold bullion, most likely bars."*

"Oh, good morning sweetheart," Lorie said, seeing Emily come in and muting the tv.

"Anything I need to know about?" Emily asked, referring to the news.

"Nope," her mother said, rinsing off some breakfast dishes. "All they've been talking about is this armored car that was knocked off the highway up near Raleigh. Nothing local. Unless you think you're stealing gold now too."

"You're up," her dad said, snapping out of his own trance. "How do you feel?"

"I'm fine," she said softly. "My head hurts a little but, I'm okay I guess. What did I . . . did I . . .? Can Grant go watch cartoons while he eats?"

"Yeah," Grant exclaimed, waiving his milky spoon in the air.

"I guess so," said her mom. "Go on. Take your bowl with you. But do not spill a drop a milk on the carpet!"

The boy slipped off his stool and carefully took his Fruit Loops into the living room. Lorie looked back at her daughter with concerned eyes. "Are you sure you're okay babe?"

"Yeah mom, I'm fine," she said. "How bad was I, dad?"

"Emily we've talked about this," he said, standing. "You can't think like that. *You* weren't bad. You can't control this thing."

"Okay, but," she started. "I'm remembering some of it. I saw someone I know. A kid from school."

"Em, for now I think it's just best you try not to remember," Adam said. "The less you know the better. I did meet your friend Morgan though."

"What?" Emily asked. "Morgan was there?"

"Yes, and thank God for her," he said. "She saved both our butts. I think I'll let her explain though. I'm not sure I even could."

"Can I just stay home today?" Emily asked. "I don't want to deal with kids at school today."

"Normally you know I'd say yes," her dad answered with a pained expression. "But today I think it's best you go and try to act normal."

Adam Morrison was concerned that when Tate Billings was found, if he hadn't already been, there would be a lot questions. He thought it best to make sure everything appear normal.

What he didn't know was that Tate's body was never going to be seen again. As far as the world was concerned, Tate would forever be simply another missing person. With an absentee father and drunk mother, it wouldn't be difficult to convince everyone he had just run away.

"It's that bad?" Emily asked, staring at her dad.

"You'll be fine, Em," he said. "Just go get ready. We need to leave in about twenty."

That morning at school actually went pretty normal. No one seemed even a bit concerned about Tate's absence. The odds were his mother hadn't even noticed. She was rarely awake when he left. His friends figured he had just ditched school to stay home, get baked, and play Madden all day. It wouldn't be the first time.

Morgan sought Emily out by her locker but was nice enough not to ask a bunch of questions. "Are you okay?" was her only inquiry.

"I'm fine," Emily said quietly, avoiding eye contact. It was bad enough that Morgan knew her secret, but now her new friend had seen firsthand what she was capable of. That was hard to process. Would she even want to be her friend anymore, now that she'd seen the truth? "I think so anyway."

"If you need to lay low," Morgan said, "you can always come hang at the shop after school. You definitely won't see anyone from school."

"Thanks," Emily shrugged.

"When it happens," Morgan started gingerly, "you're really not driving, are you?"

"Nope," Emily said. "I'm barely a passenger. I'm more like the passed out drunk girl in the back seat."

"Shit," Morgan said. "But, I think I've found a way to help with that. If you're interested. I won't do anything without permission. But I've been reading a lot about telepathic healing and psychic transference. I can explain later, but I think might be able to help unlock some controls for you."

"Really?" Emily asked, pretending she understood what any of things Morgan had just said meant. "Maybe. I just, I don't want to talk about it here."

"Fair," said Morgan, backing off. "Sorry. I just want to help. If it's okay. I don't know if there's a cure, but, I want to do something."

"It's fine," said Emily putting a hand up. "I appreciate it. Just, *later.*"

"Of course," said Morgan, understanding. She pulled something out of her shoulder bag and held it out. It was a string of beads. They were black and white quartz. There were four colored stones in the middle. "But let me give you these. I wanted to give them to you last night."

"Morgan, you don't have to give me anything," said Emily.

"I know," she said. "But this might help. It's Tourmaline quartz. That wards off bad energy. Figured you could use that. That one that looks like jade is actually *Prehnite*. It calms the mind. The dark purple one is *Charoite*. It's supposed to give you peace and wisdom. The salmon looking one is *Morganite*. It helps heal emotional trauma. I know that's a leap on my part, but it can't hurt, right?"

"What about the lavender and white one?" Emily asked.

"That's *Rhodonite*," Morgan answered. That helps to understand natural gifts, and how to control them."

"You think what I have is a gift?" Emily scoffed.

"Maybe," Morgan shrugged sheepishly. "You have to admit it's pretty powerful. You just have to get it under control first. I'll help. But we can talk about it later."

"I've never thought about it that way," Emily said. "I doesn't feel like a gift."

Emily took the beads and wrapped them around her wrist. Morgan helped clasp the bracelet.

"This is beautiful," Emily said. "Thank you." She gave Morgan a quick hug.

That afternoon Emily walked with Morgan to the Sacred Flame shop. They purposely didn't talk about the night before. Morgan was ranting about their "fascist" U.S. History teacher who "needed to retire" since she was fairly certain he must have tutored the Nazi torturer Joseph Goebbels himself.

"Can I ask you something?" Emily said when there was a lull in Morgan's tirade. "It's personal."

"Sure," Morgan nodded. "I don't mind."

"Where is your dad?"

"Oh, my dad?" Morgan repeated as if it were a confusing question, but not at all offensive. "He's in California, I think. Maybe it's Oregon. One of those."

"You think?" Emily asked. "Do you not talk to him? Are they divorced then?"

"Oh no," said Morgan. "My mom and my father were never married. He's actually very cool. We just don't really talk to him much. I got a postcard last year that he married some guy."

"Oh," said Emily, surprised.

"I know right," said Morgan. "A postcard. Like what century is this again?"

"But your dad is gay?" Emily said. "When did he come out? Was it hard for your mom?"

"Not at all," said Morgan. "My parents didn't actually have a relationship. My mom chose him. He was a friend to the coven. Plus he's really smart. Obviously." She paused and pointed to her head.

"He's also packing a pretty huge penis, according to my mother. Obviously, that didn't really help me, but I guess if I'd been a boy."

"Morgan!"

"What?" she laughed. "My mother is very open with me. It's a good thing. I'd rather that than be sheltered and lied to. She also said he had strong psychic abilities which was another reason she picked him."

"Oh, you mean besides the big dick?" Emily laughed.

"I mean, she weighed both attributes pretty equally, but yeah," Morgan laughed. "It's probably where I got my gift. I'm also developing a theory that big dicked fathers create *big boobed* daughters, but there's no real science behind it, yet."

"Hmm," Emily said, looking down. "I guess my birth father must've been pretty unimpressive down there."

"Yours are perfect," Morgan blurted out, then immediately felt embarrassed. It was like she'd basically just announced she'd looked. "I mean, they're good. They're normal. These things kill me somedays. If they get any bigger I'll need a back brace when I'm 30."

They both stared down at their chests and then broke out in laughter.

"You said your birth father," Morgan said. "So you are adopted then?"

"Yeah, if you couldn't tell by the fact that my dad's almost an albino," she answered. "Never knew either of my *biologicals.* My mom and dad got me as a baby. I was literally left at a church one night."

"Dang."

"Yeah," Emily nodded. "I was a baby in a basket. No note or anything. Almost Biblical, huh? Except for the werewolf child part."

"Well, technically there is a werewolf in the Bible too," said Morgan.

"What?" Emily coughed.

"I mean, it doesn't actually use that word," Morgan went on. "Modern church folk would never accept it, of course, but King Nebuchadnezzar of Babylon suffered from lycanthropy too. *'He was driven from men, . . .his body was wet with the dew of heaven, till his hairs were grown like eagles' feathers, and his nails like birds' claws.'*"

"The modern church tries to twist it," Morgan continued. "They write it off as a nervous breakdown. They left out some of the original text, particularly about attacking farmers and livestock. Eating their hearts and lapping up the blood."

"Seriously?" Emily asked in shock. "What happened? Did they kill him?"

"No," she said. "According to the Bible, God fixed his craziness and one day he just came back. But he was never *cured*. According to other texts, Nebuchadnezzar ruled as the only Werewolf King in recorded history. He learned to control the wolf. It was probably an effective way to deal with traitors and enemies."

"How did he control it?" asked Emily. "How can anyone control this thing?"

"With help," said Morgan matter-of-factly. "With someone who can enter their mind, and help them put a leash on the beast. Nebuchadnezzar had his court sorcerers. You've got me."

"Can you really do that?" Emily asked. "I mean, have you worked with werewolves before?"

"Uh, clearly not," said Morgan, chuckling. "But I did stop you from killing Tate the other day in the lunchroom."

"Yeah but I just killed him last night instead," Emily said.

"I'm short," Morgan answered sheepishly. "I don't peddle fast. Tate was dead either way. If you hadn't killed him, Sophie Broussard would have drained him dry. And I've heard she likes to take her time and really draw it out. There are rumors that she hangs victims in her pantry and feeds off them slowly."

"Bullshit," said Emily.

"Believe what you want," said Morgan. "At least you put him out of his misery quickly. As well as all the victims he's bullied for years. Including me."

When they reached Heron Square, Morgan went straight to the shop. Emily volunteered to make a run to what Morgan described as the "hippy coffee roaster" across the street called *Uncle John's Bean*.

As soon as she entered, Emily was greeted by a hand-painted mural covering an entire wall depicting the Grateful Dead playing Soldier Field in Chicago. A small dedication said it was painted from a photo the owner had snapped at the Dead's last show with Jerry Garcia.

Emily thought he looked a bit like a cooler version of Santa Claus, in a dark blue t-shirt and bright red pants, playing with his red guitar. Morgan's mom probably thought he was hot, she chuckled to herself.

And as if the painting were alive, a live recording of the Grateful Dead song "Friend of the Devil" played from a cassette inside a boombox behind the counter.

Emily had only seen a radio like this at her grandmother's house in Albuquerque. A piece of tape stuck to the cassette read "Philly '79" in fading, hand-scrawled ink.

The owner of the shop appeared from the back, letting the smell of roasting coffee beans escape and fill the shop with an intoxicating aroma. It was almost overwhelming to Emily's overdeveloped sense of smell.

The coffee shop owner wasn't too far off from Santa, or Jerry Garcia, himself. He could pass for an African American doppelganger of either, in a tie-dyed *Free Tibet* shirt covered in coffee stains. But he had the thick graying beard and hair.

"Namaste," he said when he saw Emily. She fought the urge to roll her eyes, because his warm smile made her think he was actually sincere. "I'm Kwame. What can I get for you?"

Emily looked up at the three chalk boards hanging above the counter that listed the house specialties, surrounded by hand drawn artwork of birds and exotic flowers. The artistry was incredible – especially for simple chalk. The colors were vivid and the details so painstakingly perfect.

"That's beautiful," she said, noticing him smiling at her.

"Thank you," Kwame nodded humbly. He pointed out that he decorated the boards himself, every morning. He referred to the entire store as his own work of art. Including the coffee.

"You're new to the area, aren't you?" Kwame asked. "I saw you walking with Morgan."

"Yeah," Emily said. "She's been showing me around. She's nice."

"Morgan is good people. Likes a latte with fresh ground cinnamon. And likes Loreena McKennitt and Etta James, so I like her. She and her mom keep the neighborhood safe. We need more like them."

His eyes twinkled when he talked. For a moment Emily wondered if he was a witch too. Or, was it wizard? Whatever male witches were called. Kwame instantly struck her as someone that truly appreciated life and understood living in the moment.

Emily liked him at once. So much so she didn't notice a big black pick-up truck drive past the shop window.

A few minutes later back at The Sacred Flame, Morgan was shelving some new books her mother had ordered when she heard the chime of the door opening.

"I'm back here Emily," she called out. "You can look at whatever. Or just chill behind the counter with Neil if you want. Whatever."

Emily didn't respond.

Morgan raised an eyebrow. She hastily put the books into a random empty space and walked up to the front of the store.

She was immediately startled by a mountain of a bearded human being wearing sunglasses in the dark store.

Luther was sporting his typical uniform of a tight dress shirt – this one a dark red – and a leather vest. His sleeves were rolled midway up his forearms, as far as they would go revealing his sleeves of tattoos.

A thin young woman with mocha skin and wild curls half-covered by a silk scarf stood behind him, her back to them both, looking at ritual candles. She wore gray leggings and black boots. She didn't need to turn around for Morgan to know it was Sophie Broussard.

Sophie had never stepped a foot inside their shop before. In fact, Morgan had never seen Sophie outside of Lune De Sang. It seemed very unlikely that her appearing today, after last night's encounter, was a coincidence. It made Morgan very nervous, but she prayed it didn't show.

Sophie turned and smiled at Morgan, peering over large designer sunglasses. She wore shiny bright red lipstick and whiter teeth Morgan had never seen, especially in the south.

"Hello Morgan," she said. "It's so good to see you again."

"What are you doing here?" Morgan snapped.

"Can't a girl just shop for enchanted candles?" Sophie asked with a shrug. "I've never been in here before. I don't get off the island much, you know."

"Yet you do still manage to get out," said Morgan, implying the last night's excitement.

"A girl's got to stretch her legs now and then," Sophie smiled, taking off her glasses. She closed her eyes and pinched the bridge of her nose. "My fucking eyeballs are still throbbing, thanks to you. It's nice in here though. By the way, where is your new friend? I don't smell her."

"You touch Emily and I will fry you, bat bitch," Morgan sneered raising her hands. "I've been preparing to run into you for a while now."

"Witch please," Sophie smiled. She looked to Luther. "You know I've been dying to say that since I got out of the car. I'm not looking for another fight with you, witchy poo, or little Miss Moonlight. Last night got out of control, for everyone."

"Not for me," said Morgan. "If I had lost control, you wouldn't be standing here."

Luther took a step toward her with a grunt. Morgan immediately stepped back.

"No, Luther," Sophie said. "It's fine. She's just protecting her friend. I get it. Although I'm not really sure you know how to kill me, or that you really would."

"What makes you think that?" Morgan asked.

"Solidarity," Sophie smiled. "We're girls. And we're freaks. You, me, and . . . Emily, is it? We're the three oddballs in town. We may be different – *very different* – but last night it occurred to me that it's nice to know I'm not alone. Don't you agree?"

"Depends on my choices," said Morgan. "Emily is cool. She's not here to mess with you, so leave her alone."

"I wasn't looking for trouble with her either," Sophie said. "In fact, technically, she's the one who interrupted my meal last night."

"You sure you weren't baiting her?" Morgan asked, squinting through her glasses.

"What are you insinuating?" Sophie asked. "I was hunting for my own damn pleasure. The only one I baited was that preppy dipshit. How in the hell could I have known your girl would come flying over the fence, all fur and slobber? Believe me, no one was more surprised than me."

She paused and bit her finger. "Well, except for Tate, I suppose."

"Then why are you looking for her?" Morgan asked, still not convinced.

"I don't know," Sophie said coyly. "I'm intrigued. There's another monster in town. We ought to get to know each other. Maybe we can help one another."

"Vampires and werewolves don't help each other," Morgan said. "I've read the histories. Your kind saw to that."

"That was way before my time," said Sophie, "I'm not interested in all that mess. I have no blood feud with Emily or anybody else. Times have changed, and we monsters need to stick together. We need each other."

"Need each other?" Morgan repeated. "You don't seem to need anyone or anything up in that big house."

"That's true," Sophie nodded. "I do keep myself locked down

pretty comfortably. But something's changed recently. I've been sensing it on the wind. There's something new on the island, and I don't mean her. For over a year I've sensed it, but since Emily got here, it's like it *woke up*."

The bell above the door rang as it was pushed open. Emily walked in holding two carboard coffee cups about to speak when she noticed Sophie and her bodyguard standing there. Her mind began flashing moments of the night before, as if piecing the broken stained glass shards back together.

She recognized this girl, and not just from seeing her standing on her porch that first day they rolled into Lune De Sang. She froze.

"Shit," was all she could manage to say.

"Hi Emily," Sophie spoke with an exaggerated kindness. "Don't worry, it's all good. I promise. I'm not here for trouble. Right Morgan?"

"Um, so she says," Morgan answered after a beat. "At least for the time being."

"Then what do you want?" Emily demanded, crossing the room along the wall to stay away from her. She set the drinks on the counter and moved in front of Morgan.

"Look girl, last night was bad all around," said Sophie. "I lost control. And I'm guessing by the way you fight that the wolf is still new to you. I don't want to hurt you."

"But you're a vampire," Emily said. "That's what we're supposed to do right? Morgan gave me a book. We're supposed to hate each other. That's why we fought last night isn't it? Wait, did we fight?"

"Wow, I hit you hard," Sophie mused.

"She doesn't retain the wolf's memories," Morgan snarled at the vampire.

"Interesting," Sophie smiled. "I wouldn't call it a fight. We tussled. I think it's fair to say we just surprised each other. And wouldn't you know, it was over a stupid boy? Such a cliché. But in our defense, we both just wanted to *eat* him."

"Your dad shut the fight down pretty quick," Morgan piped in. "Popped three rubber bullets into her dome."

"Alright don't get carried away," said Sophie. "He slowed it down. But don't sell yourself short, witchy woman. Your little *sunrise on-demand* spell really did the trick. If I were a petty person, I'd get you back for that."

"What did you do?" Emily asked, turning to Morgan who just sort of shrugged bashfully.

"The point is I couldn't sleep all day," said Sophie. "We shouldn't be fighting. You, me, and even the Kitchen Witch here. We're too powerful for middle school drama. We should be watching each other's back."

"Against what?" Emily asked.

"Every Tate Billings in the world," Sophie answered. "Among other things. Think about it. We could make this place better for ourselves, and by default, everyone else. That fuckboy Tate was making girls miserable for too long.

Thanks to us, that's no longer an issue."

"That's a pretty cold way to look at it," said Morgan.

"Who are you kidding?" Sophie asked. "You hate most people. I can smell it on you."

"She has a point," Emily added.

"Okay true," Morgan conceded. "But I haven't killed anyone. Yet. It's not our way."

"But you could," said Sophie.

"Of course I could," Morgan snapped. "But I haven't, so let's not lose sight of that."

"I'm just saying an alliance of sorts could be good for all of us," said Sophie. "We don't have to kill anyone. Well, yes, we do by very nature of what we are - vampire here, werewolf girl there. We have to feed. Can't get around it. But I've come to extend an olive branch after last night's misunderstanding."

"That's one word for it," said Morgan, rolling her eyes.

"I'm just saying," Sophie's eyes widened, "there are alternatives to stalking the townsfolk. My confidant Luther here has made certain arrangements with local bartenders, ambulance drivers, and members of law enforcement. Last night was the first time I've hunted for myself in a few years, but you don't see me going hungry." She patted her firm, flat tummy.

"We've just found a loophole to ensure that my meals are a

little more deserving," Sophie continued, nodding toward Luther. "More often than not anyway. It takes away some of the rush, like feeding lions frozen beef in the zoo, but it fulfills the need."

"Are you offering to get kills for Emily?" Morgan asked.

"I'm offering to share," said Sophie. "This town has plenty of bad people to go around."

"It's not that simple for me," said Emily. "I can't control it. When the urge comes, it completely takes over. It pushes me out of my own brain."

"It won't for long," Morgan offered. "I'm going to help you with that, remember? I hate to say it, but this actually isn't a bad idea Emily. Could keep you out of trouble. Might even help you find control."

"See," Sophie said. "The witch is right. Morgan can help you find control over your gift at my house where it's safe. And in the meantime, we can feed in private, knowing we're not putting the good citizens in danger."

"*Excuse me,*" Luthor cleared his throat. "You sure that's a good idea?"

"What are you afraid of Luther?" she asked sarcastically. "That they'll see the casket I sleep in?"

"You told me she hit you like a fucking truck last night." He looked over at Emily. "No offense kid. Sophie, you sure you want that in your living room? What if she flips and you can't stop her? And let's not forget the little one left you with a hell of a sun burn."

"Little one?" Morgan huffed.

"Relax big guy," Sophie cuffed him on the shoulder. "They're just monsters like me."

"No, he's got a point," Emily said. "Even if you're being sincere, there's always a chance things could go south. I could lose control. We might fight again."

Sophie stepped closer to Emily and Morgan.

"Maybe," she said. "But I think everything will be fine," You'll be able to satiate the beast, and keep it from running amok, clawing and biting the general public. You'd be protecting the innocent from danger, including your dear daddy."

"What about my dad?" Emily's eyes lit up, angered by the mere mention, and stepped forward.

"Girl relax," said Sophie. "I'm just saying, how long do you think he can get away with following you out at night to clean up the mess? He's going to get caught if it keeps up, and for what it's worth, that man is too fine to go to prison."

"Eew," said Emily. "That's my dad."

"So?" Sophie shrugged. "He's not mine. I'm just saying he's cute. I like them older. Although technically, I'm the older one. But he could still be my *daddy*."

"Alright stop," Emily insisted, waiving her hands. "I'll agree to whatever weird, mutant girl power pact you want. Just do

NOT talk sexually about my father. That's fucking gross!"

"Fine," Sophie chuckled with a sigh. "You're really no fun at all, are you?"

Chapter 10

Perhaps the saddest truth about the death of Tate Billings was that it took two days for anyone to realize he was missing. It wasn't until one of his buddies stopped by Tate's house after school the second day he didn't show up that Tate's own mother learned he hadn't been seen in days.

She wasn't even aware that he hadn't been home. They rarely ate together and she wasn't the type of mom who tucked her son in at night.

On Friday morning when Dr. Morrison pulled up in front of the school to drop off his daughter, there were police cars lining the front of the building. Parents and students were standing in huddled groups, some being interviewed by police officers and detectives.

Adam knew exactly what they were talking about. His hands tightened on the steering wheel and he took a deep breath.

"Okay sweetheart," he said from the side of his mouth, as if a cop might somehow hear him inside the Prius. "This is what we talked about. It's time to see how normal you can act. Someone must've finally found that kid's body."

"I'll be fine," she said, trying to reassure him. "I don't really remember anything so it's not like I can slip up and give myself away if they talk to me. What would I say, anyway? I'm a werewolf and I tore him to pieces? If anything they'd arrest me on suspicion of drugs."

"That's not funny Em," Adam shot back, but then quickly broke into a grin. "Okay, it's a little funny. And you have a point. Just stay cool. You'll be fine."

"I'm a long way from fine daddy," she said. "But I will."

"So," Adam started, changing the subject, "do you need me to pick you up this afternoon, or are you going to your friend's magic shop again?"

"It's not a magic shop dad," she said, rolling her eyes and letting out an awkward giggle. "I don't know. We might go there, or . . . she might come back to the island.

"Really?" Adam asked, with a double-take of surprise. His daughter had never invited a friend over. Not in years. "To our house?"

"Is that okay?" Emily asked, strangely nervous.

"Yeah, of course," he said, suddenly realizing he was acting sort of strange about his daughter taking an interest in a fellow young person. "No, really, it's great that you've made a friend. And one that can fight off vampires. Never thought I'd say that one."

"Okay, whatever, weirdo," she said. "I'll just text you when we figure it out."

"Great," he said. "Perfect." He watched her hands fumbling with her phone. "You good?"

"Yeah, I'm fine," she answered.

"You and Morgan really are becoming good friends, huh?" he said, more as a question.

"Yeah," she said, rolling her eyes again. "Why did you say it like that?"

"I don't know," he answered. "I'm just . . . you didn't have many friends in New Mexico."

"Yeah well, Morgan is almost as weird as I am," Emily said. "It's nice not being the only freak around. And as you said, she did save my life."

"Yeah, good point," he said. "I still get a knot in my gut knowing that thing is out there somewhere?"

"I wouldn't worry about it," said Emily, then quickly thinking she shouldn't have said anything.

"Why?" he asked. "Emily, there's a damn vampire somewhere on our island. And she already almost killed us."

"I get it," she said, wanting to get out of the car and end the conversation. Her dad probably wouldn't love knowing she and Morgan had recently had coffee with said vampire chick at the bookstore. "But I mean, I did interrupt her meal. Okay, I have to go in now, dad."

Emily leaned in and kissed him on the cheek, then quickly got out of the car and rushed away toward the school before he could say anything else.

Inside, the hallways were full of police officers in blue uniforms talking to students and teachers, jotting down statements on notepads. Emily had almost made it to her locker when two men in suits stepped out in front of her.

The taller black gentleman with a mustache and graying goatee in a dark suit flashed a wallet with a shiny badge and some form of official identification with his picture. It was legit out of a cop show.

"Miss Morrison?" he asked.

"I, uh, yes," Emily said. "I'm Emily Morrison."

"My name's Detective Will Akuna." He nodded to his partner, a slightly chubby white detective in a gray suit and orange tie with a pen behind his ear, tucked into his sweaty, curly red hair. "This is Detective Torrance. We'd like a few minutes of your time, if that's alright."

"What's going on?" Emily asked as innocently as she could feign. "Is something wrong?"

"Please," Akuna said, gesturing toward an empty classroom beside them. "It's best we sit down."

Emily stepped into the room and the two detectives followed her, shutting the door. The slight slam made her jump. She felt her heart rate elevating. This was probably a bad scenario, locked in an empty classroom with two cops.

Without seeming too obvious, she tried to take a couple calming breaths to reset her nerves. She took a seat in a desk at the front of the room. Torrance leaned on the counter where the science teacher usually sat.

Akuna grabbed a loose chair and turned it around, straddling it. This guy really did learn to be cop from the movies, she thought, stifling a nervous chuckle.

"So, I don't know if you've heard yet," Akuna started, "but one of your classmates has gone missing."

"Missing?" she said. "Who?"

"Tate Billings," Akuna answered. "Nobody has seen him since Wednesday. His school bag, his wallet, all his things are still in his room. All that's missing is his cell phone and a new pair of sneakers."

"Dang, that's terrible," said Emily. "I didn't really know him though."

"No?" Akuna squinted at her.

"I just started here this week," she answered. "My family just moved here actually. I know who he is, but that's about all."

"Okay," said Akuna. "It's weird though, because we were told you were seen speaking to Tate just the other day. In fact, you might be one of the last people he interreacted with before he left school that day."

"Who told you that?" Emily asked, slowly switching from nervous to irritated.

"Two of his friends," said Akuna. "They said they were there with him when it happened, in the lunch room. You sure about what you're telling us?"

"Oh, wait," she said. "Was that when he called me a, what was it? Oh yeah, *a fucking weirdo* who doesn't belong here. And his asshole buddies guffawed like orangutans. Did they tell you that?"

"You seem angry, Miss," Torrance finally spoke from behind Akuna.

"I am a little, *Mister*," she said. "Yes, I did have an encounter with Tate. I didn't ask for it, or provoke it. I guess he just decided to target me to make his friends laugh. He was a bully. I've dealt with them all my life. White kids used to tell me to go back to the reservation. So honestly, detectives, I don't know a damn thing about where Tate is, and I don't care either."

"Alright then," said Akuna, nodding his head. "We just wanted to confirm that he interacted with you and see if he might've said anything or done anything to indicate he was going to take off."

"*Take off?*" Emily repeated, cocking her head. Didn't they know he was dead?

"I'm guessing he got sick of his parents," Akuna spoke, lowering his voice. "His mother's an alcoholic wreck, if I'm being honest with you, and his dad's a hotshot politician who's never around. Tate's another angry young white boy that wasn't hugged enough. I'm sure he'll pop up when he runs out of cash. But his daddy's a VIP so we have to do this."

Akuna leaned in closer and raised an eyebrow. "Truth is, I don't care where he is either. But it's my job to ask."

Emily realized this detective was being honest with her, and maybe he wasn't a bad guy after all. He was just doing his job. And it didn't seem like they actually suspected her of anything.

"Look, I'm sorry," she said. "I guess I'm still a little bit sensitive about Tate after the other day."

"Hey, I hate rich white bullies too," Akuna smiled.

The detective noticed his partner giving him a disapproving look, as if he was being too candid with this young girl. He switched back to a more authoritarian tone. "So, you're sure you don't know where Tate is?"

"Nope, no idea," she answered. "We only ever spoke that one time and it wasn't what you'd call a heart-to-heart."

"Okay then," said Akuna, standing up. "Thanks for your time Miss Morrison. We have your statement. You can head to class. We appreciate your cooperation."

Emily nodded and collected her backpack and her black hoodie and walked out with a nod. Akuna looked at his partner with a shrug.

"Nice kid," he said. "You know this is a waste of our time, right?"

"You don't think she knows anything?" Torrance asked.

"What do you think?" Akuna asked. "She helped him? Did you see her eyes? She wouldn't cover for this kid. She hates him. If anything she might kill him, but we were assigned to work a missing person, not a homicide. I say we're done here."

"Teenagers," said Torrance with an apathetic shrug. "So testy these days. I blame all the screens. And that Bieber kid."

After school, Emily and Morgan hooked up on the steps and made the walk to Sacred Flame. They shared their experiences of being questioned by *Akuna "and Matata"* as Morgan affectionately renamed them. They both concurred that it seemed like the cops weren't even considering that Tate could be dead, at least for the time being.

"They'll have to at some point," Morgan said. "Somebody will find his body sooner or later. It's going to start stinking."

"Ugh, Morgan," said Emily, horrified.

"What?" she said. "It's just the truth. But I guess we'll just count our blessings for now."

"Even when they do find him, I don't think either of us needs to worry," Emily offered. "Back in New Mexico, most of my *incidents* were chalked up to wild animal attacks. I mean, there were a lot of animals out there that could tear a man apart."

"Yeah, well, we're a little short on mountain lions and

coyotes," said Morgan. She peeled off the long sleeved shirt she was wearing, revealing a black tank top with a colorful Lisa Frank unicorn print.

It was a cute, playful shirt, Emily thought. Not what she expected on someone who could be so salty and serious.

"Even wild animals can't deal with this damn humidity," Morgan said. "Every time I think it doesn't bother me, my thighs start chafing!"

"Still, when they see the state of his body," Emily continued, "they're definitely not going to think a teenage girl was responsible."

A week went by, and nothing more came of the disappearance of Tate Billings. Aside from a uniformed officer parked outside the front door of the school all day, every day, everyone seemed to go on with their lives.

Emily and Morgan were now hanging out after school like a daily routine. They were shocked that no one had discovered Tate's remains. There was nothing on the news. Nothing online.

Morgan had even been checking actual newspapers just in case. It didn't make sense. What if someone was covering it up, she wondered?

"Why would they though?" Emily asked her.

"To prevent a panic or something," Morgan said thoughtfully. "Or maybe to keep his parents out of trouble. His father is a prominent politician and not knowing your kid had vanished for two days seems more than a little bit like negligence. But this is the age of smart phones and social media. How could anyone keep something this grisly quiet for long?"

"I think we need to go look," Emily said.

"What?" Morgan asked. "Go back to the house? The scene of the . . . whatever it was? Are you crazy?"

"I'm not sure most days," Emily smiled. "But this is killing me. I have to know if his body is still there."

"And get caught?" Morgan demanded. "No way."

"What if we just casually walk past the house," Emily offered. "Come on, Morgan. At least we'll know for sure if anybody else knows he's dead."

"I don't like this plan," Morgan said. But she acquiesced. The truth was, the not-knowing was killing her too.

That afternoon, the girls rode back to Lune de Sang and the Morrison house in her dad's Prius. They made up a story about looking for starfish on the beach, and walked around the island to Delisle Street. From four houses away, they could see the For Sale sign hanging in the front yard.

Someone had absolutely been there since the night Tate died. They exchanged worried glances.

"What in the actual fuck?" Morgan started.

"I don't know," said Emily knowing exactly what she was thinking. "Is there any possible way they just put that sign up without looking in the backyard?"

Morgan stared at Emily for a second. "I never want to make you feel different or weird," she said. "But you are a werewolf. If there's a rotting body back there, wouldn't you be able to smell it?"

Emily didn't know whether to be offended or laugh. But then thought, Morgan actually had a point. She sniffed hard at the air.

"Nothing weird," she said. "Or gross. All I smell is the chlorine from the pool. But can we really go by that?"

"Nope," Morgan said, walking toward the house without hesitating. "Looks like there's only one way to know now."

"I thought you said this was crazy?" Emily asked. "That we could get caught at the scene and all that. The police could be watching the house right now, waiting to see if the killer comes back. We don't want to be attached to this."

"Yeah, I know," said Morgan. "But we're here now. And I can't go home without confirmation one way or another. Besides, our presence would be circumstantial at most."

"Umm," Emily shook her head. "Watched a lot of *Law & Order*, have we?"

"My mom," said Morgan opening the gate slowly. "She's obsessed with it. I hear that stupid *ka-chunk* sound all night long. Even if someone catches us here, they've got nothing."

"What about fingerprints or something?" Emily asked.

"I didn't touch anything," said Morgan. "The gate was open when I got here, and you had paws at the time, not fingers."

When the girls entered the backyard they couldn't believe what they saw. It looked completely undisturbed. The patio was clean. The lawn was cut. The pool water clear and blue.

"Okay, now I'm freaking out," said Emily.

"Who would clean up the body and not report it?" Morgan added. "You're probably lucky you don't remember because, *girl*, you left a mess."

"Do you think Sophie did it?" Emily asked.

"Why would she do that and not tell us?" Morgan asked.

"Maybe she came back to feed on his remains," Emily guessed. "Is that a thing they do? Never mind, that's gross. Maybe she just didn't want the attention that kind of discovery would bring to the island."

"I guess it's possible," said Morgan. "Doesn't seem like her style though. Next time she stops by, we'll have to inquire. But let's get out of here."

"Speaking of next time," said Emily, "I told her we'd come over tomorrow night."

"*We* who?" Morgan asked, looking at her with dismay. "What do you mean tomorrow night? Like a sleepover?"

"You can start working on unlocking my brain, or however you put it," Emily said. "I don't know how long I have until the next time. If you really think you can do something, I want to get started." She gestured around at the clean yard. "I can't handle this craziness much longer."

Chapter 11

The following afternoon they left school and headed for
Sacred Flame, as usual. When they reached the shop, the girls
headed upstairs to the apartment that Morgan shared with her
mother.

While Morgan had been to her house a couple times now, this
was the first time Emily had actually seen her friend's
residence. They usually just hung out downstairs in the shop
while Morgan worked.

Aside from a plethora of candles on any and every flat surface
available, Emily was struck by how incredibly normal it
seemed.

There was a blue sectional sofa and a rocking chair. A coffee
table with a few books on witchcraft, but also some knitting
magazines. The dining area housed two wall-length
bookshelves that were overflowing with books, a few weird
knickknacks, and framed photos of Morgan as a toddler.

Emily also noticed a basket full of yarn and needles and a

multi-colored scarf in progress next to the rocking chair. Morgan noticed her puzzled expression.

"My mom's obsession," she explained. "Just wait, you're probably getting a scarf for Christmas."

"You guys celebrate Christmas?" Emily asked.

"Sure," Morgan answered. "Technically we celebrate Solstice which is the 21st, before your people swiped it for your day."

"Uh, not my people," Emily said, putting her hands up. "Indian girl here, remember? Although, yes, my parents raised me Christian. Sort of. But don't even try to talk to me about people having their shit stolen."

"Fair enough," Morgan laughed. "But we do a non-religious Christmas. My mom loves the lights and the tree, and the whole peace on Earth, *yadda-yadda-yadda*. It's basically one of our tenants anyway. Plus, and this one's embarrassing so be nice, my mom is obsessed with Santa Claus."

"I'm sorry," Emily looked up, dumbfounded. "What now?"

"For real," said Morgan. "The long red robe. The beard. She's hot for Santa. And she's convinced he was probably one of us."

Morgan's bedroom was a bit more like what Emily expected. It even smelled like Morgan – a combination of patchouli and lavender. Emily took a deep breath through her nose. It was becoming a comforting scent.

The floor was covered in clothes. In fact it was almost impossible to guess what the carpet actually looked like.

There was an old dresser with multiple jewelry boxes overflowing with beads, chains, scarves, rings, and bracelets. The bed was a futon, pushed up against the wall in a corner of the room.

There were framed posters all over the walls. Artists like the Indigo Girls, David Bowie, and Janis Joplin along with more contemporary acts like Tegan & Sara, CHVRCHES, Brandi Carlile, and Christina Perri.

Morgan had also taken long pieces of colored fabrics and hung them from the center of the ceiling, billowing out to the walls, creating the illusion of a tent.

On her small desk there was a MacBook wedged between piles of books, some on witchcraft and magick, some just novels - classics and modern.

"Hold on," Emily exclaimed spying a familiar apple and white font on a black spine. She snatched it up. "Wait just a second. Fucking Twilight?"

"Screw you," Morgan grabbed it back, laughing. "I read them when I was a kid. Besides, it's good brain candy, okay?

While Morgan continued her search for something specific, Emily hung back by the desk. She happened to push the bedroom door closed a bit and was amused to see a framed poster of the main female trio from Harry Potter – Hermione, Luna, and Ginny.

At least that one makes sense, Emily thought.

"Here it is," Morgan said, finding whatever book she was

searching for and shoving it in her bag. She gave Emily an awkward look. "You sure you want to do this? I mean, you two did try to kill each other a couple days ago."

"Yeah, I think it will be fine," Emily nodded. "I just got a feeling. I know she's a bit high strung, but I think deep down she's actually cool. And lonely. I get the sense she sincerely wants to be friends with us, no matter how cool she might act."

"I know," said Morgan, holding a vial of clear liquid up in the light before dropping it in her bag. "She guards her thoughts pretty heavily but I was able to sense sincerity, beyond all her *ego*. And that's no small accomplishment on my part, if I do say so myself."

Morgan knelt beside her bed and dug around under her mattress until she pulled out a wooden rod that had been sharpened to a point on one end. "I'm still taking some old school precautions, just in case. She's going to have to earn my trust before I leave the holy water and stakes at home."

"Oh shit," Emily laughed. "Should I grab some garlic out of the fridge too?"

"Don't laugh," said Morgan. "Do you only change when there's a full moon?"

"Obviously not," Emily said.

"Exactly," said Morgan. "Not all the old wives tales are true. Garlic won't do anything to a vampire, other than make their pizza better."

"I never did understand that one," Emily said, nodding.

"There are some legends that are true," said Morgan. "The stake in the heart being one. But the trick with staking them is, once you jam it in, you have to burn the body with the stake still in place. Otherwise they could theoretically come back. Some say you should cut off the head and burning it separately, for insurance, I guess."

"I'm afraid to ask where you saw that," said Emily.

"Didn't see it babe," said Morgan, packing some extra beads. "I don't think you fully understand exactly who my mom is."

"What do you mean?" Emily asked.

"Ella Bassett, my mom, is the most famous witch alive," Morgan said, nonchalantly. "She's known throughout every magick community across the planet. She's basically the Dumbledore of our world. But she's also got enemies."

"Enemies?" Emily raised a brow. "Why? Your mom is so nice."

"Some fear her," Morgan answered. "Most just envy her power. Very few witches have ever possessed the level of magick she has."

"There is one who does," a voice said from the hall. It was Ella. She entered the room with a smile. "Her daughter."

"Mom, stop," Morgan said, turning away.

"It's true," said Ella.

She turned to Emily. "Morgan has gifts I couldn't even

imagine. I'm very proud. But of course, it also worries me. When you possess power like ours, there are always going to be those with an irrational fear of you. As my daughter grows in power and reputation, she will need eyes in the back of her head. Since the day she was born, I've known this, and I've prayed to the goddesses to send Morgan a protector. One with great power."

"Mom, I'm fine," said Morgan, feeling extremely uncomfortable with Emily in the room right at that moment.

"I just worry," said Ella. "There's an evil on that island. I've sensed it."

"We know," Morgan said. "It's the vampire. But she's fine. We've met her."

"You what?" Ella demanded. "Why would you even go near her?"

"It was my fault," Emily offered. "I sort of got in a fight with her the other night. Not intentionally. We, uh, bumped into each other. Morgan actually saved my ass."

Ella looked to her daughter for an explanation.

"The Gaelic sun spell," she told her mother sheepishly.

"It worked too," Emily enthused. "She went squealing off back into the darkness."

"Well thank the goddess for that," Ella said, shaking her head.

"She actually apologized to us," Emily said. "Well, not so much apologized, but we talked it out. She wants peace with me, and Morgan. In fact she said something similar about an evil on the island. I guess she figures having us as friends improves her chances of survival."

"And she's damn right about that," said Ella. "Still, you don't know if you can really trust her. They can't always control their thirst."

"I suppose," said Emily, "but then who am I to judge?"

"Mom!" Morgan glared.

"Oh Emily, dear," said Ella. "I didn't meant it like that. Damn me and my big mouth. I'm so sorry."

"No, I know you didn't," said Emily. "It's totally okay. I know what you meant. The good news is I'm stronger than she is. At least I think so. And I think she knows it too."

"Nevertheless, be careful," said Ella. She put her arms around Emily's shoulders and kissed her on the forehead.

At first the contact made Emily uncomfortable, but this woman had a calming presence. Something about her emanated power and love and harmony, all at once. She felt like family. "Blessed be."

Ella Bassett hugged her daughter tightly before the girls were off.

They rode bicycles across the Sayle Bridge back to Lune de Sang. Emily had borrowed Ella's bike, which never got used anymore. Emily hadn't ridden a bike in what seemed like forever. She was a little shaky at first but quickly regained the feel for it, like it had only been yesterday.

The early evening air had cooled a bit and felt good whipping through her hair. She stuck her legs out and laughed as they coasted down a small hill. Morgan couldn't help but laugh at her acting like a young child. Emily rarely let herself feel silly anymore.

The girls ate a quick dinner with Emily's family. Her mom, Lorie, made a mean spaghetti sauce and garlic bread. It was the first time Morgan had seen Emily actually eat more than a bite or two. She usually just pushed food around her plate at school.

"What are you two planning tonight?" Lorie asked them, while eyeing her son with no less than 17 full length spaghetti noodles hanging out of his mouth that he was slowly sucking back into his throat. "Grant, twirl it around the fork. You're going to choke. And you look like an ant eater."

"We're going over to a friend's house for a little while," Emily answered, making eye contact with Morgan. Neither one wanted to answer too many questions about who they'd be spending time with that night.

"A friend?" Lorie looked up. "Another one? Someone on the island?"

"Uh, yeah," said Emily.

"Who?" her dad added. "Where does she live? It is a *she*, right?"

"Yes, dad," Emily said, rolling her eyes. Morgan chuckled. "She lives across from the beach."

"Who is it?" he asked. "Have we met her parents?"

"I doubt it," Emily said, shoveling pasta into her mouth.

"Well does she have a name?" Lorie asked. "And a phone number in case we need you."

"Mom, I'll have my iPhone," said Emily.

"Her name's Sophie," Grant piped up. Both Emily and Morgan nearly choked. "I heard them talking about her in the other room."

"No, it's Stephanie," Morgan interjected. "Her name's Stephanie . . . uh, *Du Soleil*."

Emily shot Morgan a look.

"As in *Cirque*?" Lorie questioned.

"Sounds French," Adam added, before taking a bite of garlic bread. "Like everything else around here."

"Yeah, she lives on the other side of the island," Morgan added. "She comes from one of those old Lune De Sang family."

"Really?" Lorie asked suspiciously. "In other words, she's got money."

"Uh, yeah," said Morgan. "You could say that."

"Well, be home by eleven," said Adam. He turned to Morgan. "You're more than welcome to sleep here tonight, as long as your mom is cool with it."

"Thanks Mr. Morrison," she said with an awkward smile.

After dinner the girls made the short trip to Sophie Broussard's Saint Charles mansion on foot.

"Who the hell is Stephanie du Soleil?" Emily immediately chided Morgan, laughing hysterically.

"I had to cover quickly after your brother said Sophie's name," she explained. "I said it to your dad the other night."

"You did?" Emily asked. "Why would you that?"

"It wasn't like I expected us to be having a girls night out with her," Morgan said. "It just sort of came out."

The girls approached the big pink mansion and found the gate was wide open. They both held their breath.

"You sure about this?" Morgan asked.

"Come on," Emily exhaled.

They walked up the path, to the stairs and onto the sprawling porch. The big white front door had an iron knocker shaped like a Fleur-de-lis. Morgan flashed Emily a look as if to say this was their last chance to get out of there. Emily rolled her eyes. She lifted the metal ring and knocked three times.

After a moment they heard someone unlocking the deadbolt on the other side. The door swung open and there stood Luther, all meat and muscle and leather vest, with braids in his beard and earrings lining his left ear cartilage.

He was wearing his trademark sunglasses even though night had fully fallen long ago, and the house lighting didn't seem much brighter inside. They saw his eyebrows lift slightly then fall behind the lenses. He grunted.

"Sophie," he called back over his shoulder. "Your company has arrived."

Sophie appeared from the end of the hallway behind him in skinny jeans and a crop top. She had an enormous grin on her face and came running down the hall. She did not look like the undead to Emily. She looked like just another teenager.

"I still can't believe you told them to come," Luther grumbled.

"It's called an invitation, asshole," she said, slapping his arm. "Ladies, forgive him. He's not normally allowed to talk . . . *to anyone.*"

"You're the one who said they both tried to kill you the other night," he said, stepping out of the way. The girls both noticed the very large shiny knife he'd been holding behind his back. He flipped it over and slid it into a sheath on his belt. "It's your funeral. And the papers say I get this place if you ever do croak, so, have a party."

"Go find snacks for us," she ordered him.

"It's alright, we just ate," said Morgan.

"Well, just in case," said Sophie. "Drinks too. Cokes, Pellegrino, and put a Riesling on ice, just in case. You ladies feel like having some big girl drinks tonight?"

"Um, I don't know," Emily started.

"I'm in," Morgan spoke up.

"Alright," Sophie smiled, impressed. "You might be cool after all Bassett. Come on you two. Let me show you the house."

Most of the mansion was very much as would be expected. Many rooms, filled with old furniture, older art, and fragile dishes. Sophie led them up the grand staircase to the second floor where she had made more contemporary upgrades.

"I don't ever bring any townies up here," Sophie winked. "I usually make the locals stay downstairs with the dusty *white folk* antiques. Up here, this is my domain."

There was a vast media room. Sophie had knocked down three sets of walls to make one large space with an enormous 88" HD flat screen television and long black and purple leather sectional couch with 5 separate reclining sections, each with built-in cup holders.

"That's custom made," she explained, gesturing at the sofa. There were also matching leather recliners and end tables at either side of the couch. And brightly colored overstuffed beanbags were spread around all over the thick black carpet.

"I originally installed white carpet," Sophie said. "But then I learned the hard way that the combo of red wine and blood stains like a bitch."

The walls of the room were lined with framed classic horror movie posters.

"You don't feel weird about that?" Morgan asked her, pointing to a framed Dracula print.

"Who, Bela?" Sophie asked. "Hell no. He's iconic.

Besides, Dracula's the closest thing to a folk hero my kind has. I might as well embrace it, right?" She pointed at the Wolfman poster a few frames down the wall and winked at Emily. "So I guess that means that's your guy."

"That's so corny," Emily said. "Is that what I look like?"

"Not even close," said Morgan.

"She's right," said Sophie. "For what it's worth, you're terrifying. And bad ass, babe." She pointed at another movie poster across the room. "You're much closer to American Werewolf in London. But taller."

The room had a fully stocked bar and a movie theater popcorn machine. Sophie picked up a remote and pointed it at a book shelf containing a few books, including the entire Harry Potter series and a painted skull and some other odds and ends.

The entire shelving unit slowly turned out into the room and all the way around, revealing rows and rows of Blu-rays.

"If you guys want to watch a movie, I've got everything," she said. There's a closet full too. Anything I don't have, we can stream."

"Maybe later," Emily said. She felt strange about the way Sophie was treating this like just a weekend hangout with the girls.

Although she wasn't really sure what to expect on the way over, maybe she was unnerved my how shockingly normal Sophie's home was. Some part of Emily expected some gothic chamber with bodies hanging from hooks. She had pictured red candles, torture racks, and weird statues of crying angels.

This seemed like the exact room a teenager would put together, given unlimited funds and no parental supervision.

"Where is your bedroom?" Morgan asked.

"Up in the attic," Sophie responded. "I have a special rig that I hang upside down from."

Both girls just stared at her dumbfounded. Sophie could almost hear their eyelids blinking.

"I'm kidding," she said, laughing. "Shit, you two need to relax. I'm making margaritas."

"Margaritas?" Emily said.

"I'm in," said Morgan.

"Didn't you just tell your, uh, whatever he is, to chill some wine?" Emily asked.

"Yeah, I know," said Sophie moving behind the bar. "It gives him something to do. When you're that big, it's good to stay busy. If Luther sits still for too long, he might never get back up."

"So is he a," Emily started, then paused. "Is Luther like you?"

"What, a vampire?" Sophie responded. "Luther? Hell no. You

know how much blood it would take to satisfy that boy? He'd drain this island by Thursday. No, Luther is my caretaker. He looks out for me."

"You mean your *familiar*?" Morgan responded.

"Luther is far from a familiar," Sophie rolled her eyes. "Does anything about him look subservient. We have a mutually beneficial relationship."

"Where did you find him?" Morgan asked.

"Actually, he found me," she said. "About sixty years ago Luther found me floating in Lake Ponchetrain."

"What?" asked Morgan, wide-eyed. "In New Orleans? What happened?"

"I'm not really sure," she answered, pouring sour mix into a shaker. "I have this large black spot in my memory."

"How large?" Emily asked as she took a glass from Sophie. She took her first sip of the tart cocktail. The initial sour shock was followed by a warming feeling in her chest.

"Almost two centuries."

"Are you being serious?" Emily asked, almost spitting margarita.

"Pretty much," Sophie nodded. "I remember most of my childhood. We lived in a big house in New Orleans. It belonged to Levasseur. My mom played piano during his dinner parties. She wasn't a slave, mind you. She was what they called *gens de couleur libres*."

"Free people of color," Morgan translated. "Like the Anne Rice book."

"That's right," said Sophie. The story goes the old scoundrel fell hard for my mom while she was in his employ. At least, for a while. And then an angry mob stormed the house when I was around 12, and it all goes dark, until just before Luther saved me."

"You actually lived in the same house as Henri Levasseur?" Morgan marveled. "Did he, well, I don't know how to ask this. Is he the one that turned you?"

"You could say that," Sophie laughed. "He was my father."

"Levasseur was your father?" Morgan was shocked. She had known there was a family connection, but she had assumed it had been somewhere further down Sophie's ancestral line.

"Yes," Sophie laughed again. "Obviously I can't tell the townsfolk that. But it's true. The man they call a devil, and he could be, was my daddy. I just refer to him as a distant ancestor."

"What was he like?" Emily asked.

"He wasn't around much," Sophie answered. "And when he was, he kept to himself. At night he was probably out feeding. But from time to time he'd appear around dinner, and he'd be kind, and shower me with gifts. And he was protective.

You may have heard things weren't wonderful for people like me back then, particularly in the good old south. When Levasseur learned about this undeveloped island off the coast of Charleston, he got the idea to buy it and make it a safe haven for us, and anyone like us."

"You mean like a community for multiracial families?" Morgan asked.

"No, for vampires, dummy," Sophie grinned. "Though yes, I guess the other thing too. There were a number of us around New Orleans. Until the attack."

"What happened?" asked Emily. She started to feel like she was prying, which she didn't like when people did to her. "You don't have to tell me, if you don't feel like it."

"No, it's okay," said Sophie, taking a big drink. "You probably should know. History does seem to repeat itself."

"Eventually my father's secret got out and a mob stormed our house with torches, rifles, the whole nine. The bastards killed my mom. They killed the staff. They burned the house down. The last thing I remember was a rifle pointed at my face and some plantation boss saying *die devil*."

"My god," Emily whispered. "What happened? I mean, you're here so obviously you got away."

"Oh, I didn't," Sophie said, polishing off her drink. "He pulled the trigger. I can still see the flash. Then nothing. But apparently after taking bird shot to the face, I was left in the burning house. Lucky for me, the stupid redneck forgot to stake me."

"Jesus," gasped Morgan, tears forming in her eyes. She had read tales of her own ancestors being burned alive. Some as young as 8 or 9. How could anyone murder a child out of pure superstition? It was barbaric. "What happened to you?"

"I don't know how or why I woke up, but I did," Sophie said. "Eventually. Mind you, I wasn't quite the beauty queen you see before you now. Decades had passed. They'd dumped all the remnants of the house in the swamps and buried them under a thin layer of top soil."

Sophie paused. The girls saw her eyes glisten but no tears escaped.

"I don't remember anything after the gun shot," Sophie went on. "Until the day Luther found me. He saw some girl floating face down in the lake and tried to perform CPR, bless his dumbass heart. I almost bit his tongue off."

"That's horrible," Emily said, wiping her eyes. "So when your dad, Levasseur, came to Lune de Sang, he thought you were dead?"

"As far as I know," Sophie answered. "Most of the other vampires we knew in the area had been staked. I don't know if any of them ever woke up again. I got lucky. The inbreeders who staked me thought that was all it took."

"Wait," Morgan said suddenly, "I thought all the legends say when Levasseur came to Lune De Sang, he had a young girl with him. That wasn't you?"

"They do say a lot of things, don't they?" Sophie responded. "But no, that was not me girl. I was in a deep, deep sleep somewhere in the muck. If that's true, I don't know who it was. With a father like mine, anything's possible."

"Did you ever see your father again?" Emily asked.

"No, not in the flesh," said Sophie. "He returned to Europe after a century or so. He was good about moving on, blending into another world. And then at some point, he was killed. That's what they say anyway."

"But you were his daughter," Emily said. "Even if he was a vampire, didn't that mean anything to him?"

"I suppose the longer you live, the easier it is to sever emotional attachments," Sophie said. "Hell, they say he drained half of his lovers. Even the ones he loved. It just happens. But he must have felt something for me, because he left a chest filled with personal effects, including a will stating his fortune, including this house, and a castle in Europe, was all mine."

"So he knew you were still alive," Emily said.

"I think it was more of a guess," she answered. "A law firm in London sent a representative to America to determine if the lost daughter of Levasseur still lived. They, in turn, hired a bunch of mercenaries to act as private detectives and track me down, if I was in fact alive."

"Let me guess," Morgan started. "One of them has a thing for leather vests and is built like a minivan."

"Very good," Sophie grinned. "Luther was instructed that if he found me alive, he was to change that status immediately. The bankers were collecting a small fortune as custodians of the Levasseur estate. Luckily for me, the asshole is actually a big softy."

"And you've been keeping him alive ever since in return," said Morgan.

"I have to," Sophie said. "I may be 200 but I still look 19. It's helped to have *Uncle Luther* around to pass off as some kind of guardian.

"How though?" Emily asked. "If he's not a vampire, how does he still look like he's in his forties?"

"He drinks her blood," Morgan answered softly. "Doesn't he?"

"Not directly from my veins," Sophie answered, as if that made it seem more normal. "But, yes, once a year I open a vein into a glass, mix it with a nice Cabernet or Merlot, and Luther sucks it down. It's not a big deal. Vampire blood has more health benefits than wheat grass and acai. The guy hasn't even had a cold in over seventy years."

"It does more than that," Morgan said. "Doesn't it?"

"Yes," Sophie said, looking at the young witch. "It has healing powers. A couple of years after he found me, Luther took a bullet protecting me. He was lying in the street, bleeding out. I didn't know what else to do so I bit into my own wrist and squeezed blood into the bullet hole, and into his mouth. It worked. His body pushed the bullet out of the wound and he opened his eyes. Ever since, I've been mixing up my special crimson cocktail for him."

Emily gulped and looked at the glass in her hand. The liquid inside was a murky green. Probably no vampire blood hidden within. She took another sour sip.

"What about you, Moonlight?" Sophie asked. "What do you know of your past? How did you become this way?"

"No clue," she said. "I'm adopted, as you probably guessed when you saw my dad."

"Mmm, your hot dad," Sophie beamed, taking a drink.

"Don't start," said Emily with a laugh. "At least one of my biological parents was Navajo. We used to talk about getting a DNA test but, given recent changes, I'm honestly afraid. God knows what else might come up."

"Mexican gray wolf," Sophie grinned wryly.

"Native American makes sense," said Morgan. "Skin walkers. Trickster gods. They're all in-line with lycanthropy. Maybe one of them was like you. Maybe that's why they left you at that church, hoping to protect you from a family curse."

"They could've been more help to me by sticking around," said Emily. "They could've warned me. Or actually raised me and taught me how to deal with it. Don't get me wrong, I love my parents more than anything. As far as I care, they are my mom and dad. That's why I cry myself to sleep, scared I'm going to kill them in their sleep, with no power to stop myself."

"You're not," said Morgan, putting a hand on her back. "That's the reason we're here. Besides, if one or both of your parents were werewolves, who says they could control it either? Maybe they were just as afraid of killing you."

"She's got a point sweetheart," Sophie lifted her glass. "It is instinctual for some predators to eat their own young."

"We're not hyenas," Emily snapped.

"I was only making a point," Sophie explained. "Maybe they did you a solid. And you ended up the baby girl of a hot doctor and a rich mom."

"We're far from rich," said Emily. "We just got a house. And look who's talking."

"Does that little squirt I saw in the van have any secrets?" Sophie asked. "I assume he won't grow up to be another Eddie Munster?"

"The guy from Pearl Jam?" Emily asked confused.

"Good lord," Sophie rolled her eyes. "I mean, is your brother a wolf pup?"

"No, Grant is their biological kid," Emily answered. "He was a surprise. They weren't supposed to be able to have kids of their own.

"Well if we're going to make sure you don't eat that little miracle baby, you two ought to do whatever it is Sabrina here is planning quick so you can get control over this thing."

"She's right," Morgan said, glaring at Sophie. "It's probably not going to work the first time. I don't know. Obviously, I've never actually done this before."

"What do we have to do?" Emily asked.

"Sit down on a barstool," said Morgan. She rubbed at a crystal around her neck and lifted it to her lips to kiss it.

"Maybe I shouldn't have had that alcohol," Emily wondered aloud, sitting at the bar.

"Actually it might help," said Morgan. "You need to relax your mind. The less you think, the better."

"I've got better stuff than booze for that," said Sophie.

"No, I still need her somewhat lucid," said Morgan. "Not tripping balls on Mars. Now close your eyes, Em."

Emily did as instructed. Morgan placed a palm on her forehead. It instantly occurred to her this was the first time she'd ever really touched Emily's skin.

Morgan took a deep breath. She ran her finger back into Emily's smooth black hair, then slowly drew it forward again. She did this a couple times.

"I'm not really needed here, am I?" Sophie asked, feeling a bit awkward about all this hocus-pocus stuff. "I'm going to dip out. And I should probably check on Luther. Come down whenever you're done, or feel ready, or whatever."

"Good idea," said Morgan. "This is probably going to seem weird."

"Oh, *now* it's going to get weird?" Sophie smirked. She grabbed her drink and slipped out of the room.

"You'll hear my voice, but I won't be speaking," Morgan explained to Emily, ignoring Sophie. "Not out loud anyway."

"Okay," Emily nodded. "I guess my brain is in your hands."

"Are you comfortable?" Morgan's voice asked after a few

moments. "You can sit on the couch if that feels better."

"I'm fine," Emily answered.

"You don't have to speak," Morgan said. "I'm not. I'm in your consciousness. Just think it and I'll hear it."

"Um, okay," Emily spoke out loud, then stopped. *Okay*, she thought. *Is it working? Can you hear me?*

Yes, she heard Morgan laugh. *Just relax. I'm going to put you into a sleep state so I can look for something.*

Look for something?

Yes, it's complicated, Morgan said. *I need to see what the wolf sees. It's in your subconscious. I can't see it with you in the way.*

How are you going to put me in a sleep . . .?

"GO TO SLEEP," Morgan said audibly, pressing her hand against her forehead. Emily was immediately silent. She was unconscious, lost in a dream.

Morgan could sense the peace in her mind. She took the opportunity to cross over into Emily's consciousness.

She saw what seemed like a star pattern, flying towards her. The sounds of static flowing in like waves. Within seconds, it was quiet, and she knew she was inside Emily's mind.

Not literally of course. This was another plane of reality. A spiritual construct. But now Morgan had access to Emily's thoughts, and her memories. She felt a great weight of responsibility. This kind of access to another person's mind was very special, and could easily be abused. Morgan had to be sure not to overstep the permission Emily had entrusted her with.

Even if there were other questions she'd love to know answers to.

Morgan felt like she was floating down a black corridor. The air had texture. It was like pushing through water but there was none. There were flashes of light every few seconds as she moved, each in various shades of white, yellow, and blue, green. And some red.

Morgan had a sense that the red flashes were probably what she was looking for. They were memories of anger, rage, and crisis. If the memories of the wolf were still inside Emily's brain, these would likely be them.

Time was of the essence. Morgan had to look for specific memories.

She floated toward a dim red light. She grabbed at the light with her hands and cupped it like a sphere. It felt like gelatin, but at the same time empty. When she gripped the sides, Morgan was able to pull it open and bring it to her face until enveloped her.

Suddenly Morgan was in the Morrison's kitchen, and she was looking at Grant, Emily's brother, who had come running in full-bore without warning and crashed into his sister, spilling a bright ruby fruit punch all over Emily's white shirt.

That wasn't what she was looking for, but it did confirm Morgan's theory that the red lights were indeed moments of anger in Emily's past.

Morgan floated further down the corridor, but it didn't take long until something out of place caught her eye. Hidden behind a cool green aura, which Morgan knew to be a calming, comforting memory, she could see a trace of something flashing.

She gently moved the green memory blob of light away and found a brighter, pulsating red light. Morgan again held it and peered inside.

Instantly, a sound like a thousand sirens and bells and animal screams erupted in her ears. Morgan clapped her hands to her ears but it didn't help. This was not a human memory. She grit her teeth and forced herself to look again.

Against the ear-splitting cacophony, she found herself on top of Tate Billings, who's mouth opened and closed like a fish dying on the shore as blood gushed from the gaping hole in his neck where his throat had been seconds before.

The seventeen-year-old boy's eyes were filled with a fear she'd never seen on a human's face. She watched a pair of strong, hairy claws rip through layers of flesh and muscle, violently tearing them from his skeleton as he silently begged for it to end.

Then came the jarring sound as the left side of his rib cage was finally wrenched open to expose his still pumping organs, like the Jaws of Life tearing a door off a wrecked car to extract a trapped passenger.

Morgan pulled her face back out of the memory. She was

drenched in a cold sweat.

Once she caught her breath, she closed the memory back up. She glanced around frantically. She happened to notice another light, this one yellow, but with something else pulsating behind it.

Morgan drifted over and pushed away the gelatinous yellow sphere to reveal another red one loosely stuck to it. She pulled them apart, like separating two of those sticky wall-walking octopuses she used to play with as a child.

She did herself the favor of not looking into this one. It was more than likely another of Emily's more brutal memories that Morgan didn't need to witness firsthand.

It didn't make sense, but somehow, Emily's subconscious was actively hiding these violent memories behind more pleasant ones.

Maybe it was some instinctive act of self-preservation, she guessed. That would explain why Emily could never really remember becoming the wolf. Those violent moments were masked behind normal everyday recollections. At best, she could only spy traces of her hunting escapades pulsing behind her memories.

But this was only one. Morgan knew there had to be more. So, where were they?

Morgan floated further into Emily's mind. It took some time before she found another of these red memories, but when she did it was *the motherload*.

She came upon an opening in what could best be described as a cerebral hallway. A second celestial corridor, like a tunnel of stars and lights, broke away from the stream of memories. The opening was thin and harder to pass through.

"Jeez," Morgan grunted as she squeezed through the crevasse. "Em, we have got to open your mind up to big boobs. I feel like I'm trying to pass through the birth canal."

Morgan discovered a cluster of pulsing, flaring red memories. There were no other lights within this stream. She opened another; this time a violent attack behind some brick building in the desert. Teeth tearing through flesh, sinking into tight, scared muscle. The taste of blood. The smell of sweat. Morgan immediately pulled away.

This was where Emily's subconscious was storing the memories of her transformations. Morgan began gathering them in her arms like a bushel of red apples. She knew what she had to do, but she didn't love it.

"Sorry Emily," Morgan said. "When you wake up, this is really going to suck. But I think it's the only way. You can't gain control over something you can't see."

Morgan pushed her way back out of the *rage vault* she'd entered and back into the primary stream of Emily's consciousness.

As she floated back the way she'd come, she noticed the first bright red memory, the one where Emily had killed Tate Billings, snaking its way through the other colored flashes towards that secret chamber of her memory.

Morgan almost reached out to snatch it, but opted to let it slip into the secret hiding place. "You don't need that one anymore."

The witch opened her eyes. She was standing in front of Emily, with her palm still flat against her forehead. Morgan stroked the hair along the side of her friend's face.

"Emily," she said softly. "Em, you're going to wake up in a second. When you do, you're going to see things – awful things that there's no way to prepare you for. I'm sorry to do this, but it's the only way for you to gain control of the wolf. No matter what happens, I'll be right here with you."

"Emily," Morgan swallowed hard. "Wake up."

Chapter 12

The quiet girl with the long black hair opened her almond-eyes and blinked. For a moment, she saw her new friend Morgan standing in front of her and she smiled.

Then, without warning, a dozen of the most horrific, violent, gruesome memories filled her mind all at once. She was transported to every attack she'd committed in the last year. Tackling strangers to the ground, feeling their bodies ripped apart in her claws. Hearing every scream just inches from her ears. Tasting their blood and vital organs in her mouth, as if it were all happening right there in Sophie Broussard's house. Emily let out a tortured, terrified scream.

"Emily," Morgan said loudly, "I'm right here with you. These aren't happening now. They're just memories. You are safe. I'm here, and you're okay."

Emily fell to the floor, gripping her hair and gnashing her teeth. A flood of tears streamed from her tightly clinched eyes. Her body convulsed. She was struggling just to breathe.

Morgan fell to her knees beside her and wrapped her in a hug, holding her arms down at her sides. She was immediately engulfed with guilt and doubt. Had this been the wrong course of action?

"Emily, listen to me," said Morgan firmly, trying to contain the urge to cry with her. "These are things that have already happened. It's over. You're safe now. You are okay."

"No," Emily screamed. "No, I'm not okay! I did those things! How could I ever be okay?"

"What the hell is happening?" Sophie came barreling into the room. "What did you do? What's wrong?"

"I had to show her the memories," Morgan said, rocking the struggling girl in her arms. "It's the only way."

"What do you mean, the memories?" Sophie asked. "Which ones?"

"The memories of the wolf," Morgan explained. "Her brain was hiding them, storing them away in her subconscious. Probably as a defense mechanism."

"Probably a damn good one," Sophie yelled. "Why the hell would you do that?"

"It was the only way," repeated Morgan. "You think I wanted this? She can't control something she doesn't know. Now her mind is opened. Now I can help her, assuming . . .." Morgan's words trailed off.

"Assuming what?" Sophie demanded.

"Assuming this doesn't drive her insane," she said.

"Are you kidding me?" Sophie demanded. She dropped to her knees, pushing Morgan away from the girl, who was still trembling and sobbing. She cupped Emily's face in her hands.

"Now you listen to me Emily. Listen to Sophie. You're going to get through this. Look into my eyes."

She had to pry Emily's eyelids open.

The frightened girl struggled to pull away but Sophie wouldn't allow it. In these human forms, Sophie was the stronger between them. The vampire's eyes turned bright red. She peered deep into Emily's own bloodshot eyes.

"Calm down," Sophie whispered. "You will be calm. You will accept what you've seen in your mind, and accept that it is not your fault. This was done to you. There was nothing you could have done to stop it. You have cried for what happened. And now, you will get past the sadness. You will stop this crying *now*."

Just as if she'd flipped a switch, Emily stopped shaking. Her sobs were silenced and she slowly caught her breath. Sophie pulled her own sleeve foreword and wiped Emily's eyes.

"You good?" Sophie asked after a few silent moments as the girl fought to compose herself.

"Yeah, I . . . I think I am," Emily answered.

"How did you do that?" Morgan marveled.

"You think you're the only one who can play with people's

brains?" Sophie guffawed. "How do you think I've lived in this town so long without anybody asking why I never age a damn day?"

"Emily," Morgan started, "I'm sorry. I wish I . . . I'm so sorry."

"It's okay," said Emily, managing a smile. "I think I understand why. It was just overwhelming. It was worse than I could have ever imagined. Worse than any horror movie. And my dad has seen me do some of those things. How can he even look at me?"

"Dads can be weird," Sophie shrugged. "You should hear some of what mine witnessed."

"He loves you," Morgan added. "That's how. You're his daughter. He also knows that it wasn't really you. Sophie was right. You weren't in control of any of it."

"That's the thing," said Emily. She paused for a moment, staring at her hands. "It is me. At least, it's in me. My dad keeps saying he's going to cure this, but, I don't think there is a cure."

"You don't know that," Morgan tried to assure her.

"Curing it would mean killing the wolf," said Emily. "I can't kill the wolf. It's not a parasite. It's actually part of me. Like, the creatures in The Dark Crystal. If the one dies, they both die. All I can do it try to put it on a leash."

"Then that's what we're going to do," said Morgan.

"It's not all bad," Sophie spoke up. "Think about it. You've got incredible power. And I bet you never get sick, do you?"

Emily thought for a moment and shook her head no. She hadn't had so much as a cold in years. Not since the wolf first appeared.

"See, you just need to get a handle on this thing," said Sophie. "It's not the worst situation. You'd be like a super hero."

"Super heroes don't eat people," Emily rolled her eyes. "Not even the bad people."

"There's always a give and take," Sophie responded. "Make your peace with it, just as I have with my inner-demon. I take bad people off the streets, and I feed my hunger. I didn't ask for this, but we can only play the hands we're dealt."

She paused to take a sip.

"My father left me a letter before he died," Sophie continued. "On the chance that I had survived, I suppose. He wrote: *Comme le diable lui-même, je ne suis qu'un pion impuissant dans un jeu plus grand, damné pour jouer mon role."*

"Like the devil himself," Morgan began to translate.

"I am but a powerless pawn, in some grander game, damned to play my part," Sophie finished. "All we can do is survive."

"She's right Emily," said Morgan. "At least we're all together. We can help each other. We can watch each other's' backs."

"We're like a Charlie's Angels," Sophie grinned, holding out a drink to Emily, "but, you know, more like his demons."

"It's just so random," said Emily after a moment. She sat up and took a gulp of the sweet sour cocktail. She licked her lips.

"What is?" Sophie asked.

"The three of us ended up living within a mile or so of each other," Emily answered. "A vampire, a werewolf, and a witch. It's a weird coincidence, don't you think? Guess it was destiny or something."

"I wonder," said Morgan after a beat. Her brow furrowed behind her glasses. It was the first time she'd really considered it. "Now that you say that, I wonder, is it random? I've lived here all my life. Sophie, you came back to Lune de Sang right before I was born right? But we've somehow managed to avoid each other for sixteen years. Then Emily, you show up."

"No offense," Sophie said draining her own glass, "but you didn't avoid me. I stayed away from you, for fear of your mother. I knew she sniffed me out the instant I landed."

"Whatever," said Morgan. "My point is, are we sure this was coincidence. What are the odds three people like us would end up in the same tiny patch of Earth?"

"Well, I mean, it is near a big research lab," said Emily. "My dad's a scientist. I'd say that narrow's the odds somewhat."

"Meh, maybe," said Morgan. "It's just weird. My mom said she's been sensing something here on the island. Some presence."

"For real?" Sophie asked, suddenly perking up. "I've been

feeling something weird too. I just thought it was Emily."

"And my mom thought it was you," said Morgan. "But then she said she realized it was something different. A presence that came sometime after you, Sophie, but long before Emily showed up."

"You think something drew us together?" Sophie asked, raising an eyebrow.

"Morgan, come on," said Emily with a giggle. She couldn't know for sure if it was the margarita or the fact that Morgan had just been poking around inside her brain, but she suddenly felt very loose. Her brain was tingling. And she felt more at ease. This was only her second alcoholic drink in her life. And her first experience with tequila. "Maybe the goddess willed it."

"I hope you're right," Morgan said in return.

"*Sade*," Emily said, holding her glass in the air, "I need another one of these."

"Damn girl, getting all bossy now, are we?" Sophie asked. She took the glass and sauntered back to the bar, looking over her shoulder. "I'm kind of into it."

Emily looked back at Morgan. Her crazy curls were falling over her glasses. Her brow was furrowed.

Even in her somewhat impaired mental state,

Emily could tell her new friend's brain was probably obsessing over the possibility of some unknown threat pulling them all together. She wished she hadn't even brought it up.

But watching Morgan's mind work was amusing, and kind of cute. Emily spontaneously leaned forward and threw her arms around Morgan.

"Hey, what are you doing?" Morgan said, surprised, but chuckling, albeit awkwardly.

"I love that you worry, kid," said Emily, slurring her words just a bit. "But I think we're going to be okay. I mean, think about it." Emily leaned into Morgan's ear and whispered. "Until a few days ago, our biggest worry was the vampire in town, and now look."

Emily suddenly got loud again and gestured widely toward Sophie standing behind the bar mixing cocktails. "She's on our side! We're good. We're all good. We've got each other now."

Morgan blushed and looked down at the carpet. She felt her cheeks flush. She'd been trying to deny that being around Emily stirred certain feelings. Feelings she wasn't sure what to do with. But they were getting harder to deny. Emily whispering in her ear had sent those clandestine emotions, along with goosebumps, coursing through her body, and flooding to her temples.

But this was not the time, she told herself, even if there were a possibility. And it certainly wasn't the place. She could already feel Sophie's eyes burning into her with that puckish grin.

"What's wrong?" Emily asked, leaning back and giving her a cock-eyed look.

"Nothing," said Morgan, rubbing her shoulders and then pulling away. "I just hope you're right. That's all. I also don't want to be your mom, but maybe you should slow down on the tequila. It can be dangerous, even to an experienced drinker."

"She's fine," said Sophie, handing Emily another glass of the chartreuse punch over ice with a wedge of lime. "Let the girl feel good. It's not easy for people like us. Trust me. We spend the first year or two feeling like the monsters history has branded us to be. Which, I mean, I technically we are. But it's not like we asked for it."

Downstairs they heard the doorbell ring. Sophie raised an eyebrow and looked surprised. She didn't get visitors very often - not without warning – and not this late.

"You two stay here," she said with more than a little concern. "It's probably just somebody wanting me to donate to another fundraiser. I get that a lot. Luther can usually handle them, but I like to spy from the stairs. You two just hang out. You don't need anyone seeing you here and starting some neighborhood bullshit."

"For sure," said Morgan, grateful for the distraction.

"Okay, what's going on with you?" Emily asked Morgan once Sophie was out of the room. "You're acting weird. Did you see something else in my brain? Should I be worried?"

"No, nothing," said Morgan. "Seriously, it's all good. You've seen everything I found."

"Then why do I feel like you're suddenly in a hurry to get away from me?" Emily asked. "The awkwardness is real."

"I'm sorry," said Morgan. "I don't want it to be. I guess there's something overwhelming about all this for all of us."

"About what?" Emily asked. "Being friends with monsters?"

"Stop using that word," said Morgan, pushing her arm. "You're not a monster. I don't even think Sophie is. Obviously, I did. And I do still think she might have a slightly evil streak, but she's not a demon."

"Then what?" Emily asked. "Tell me."

"It's hard," said Morgan. "Until a few weeks ago, I didn't really have any friends in school. Then you showed up and it's like, I don't know, now there's someone I like being around. Someone who doesn't make fun of me, or annoy me just by their very existence."

"Don't you realize I feel the same way?" Emily said. "I was in the same situation. I didn't have any friends in New Mexico, even before I became this."

"Yeah, but," Morgan started, "it's more than that. Maybe. I don't know. It's complicated."

"What are you babbling about girl?" Emily laughed. She took a drink and pointed a finger at Morgan, while the others still clutched the glass. The green liquid sloshed around and she raised her hand. "You know what it is? I think you just think too much. You're an *overthinker*."

"Oh trust me, you have no idea," said Morgan. "I can get in

and out of someone else's brain easily, but sometimes can't get out of my own head for days. I don't know, . . . I'm just glad you moved here. Regardless of why."

"Me too, *Morg*," said Emily. She put her glass down and hugged her again. This time holding on a little longer. "You don't how good it feels to not to be so alone anymore. My parents are here, but it's not the same as having a girlfriend to help me through it."

"Girlfriend," Morgan repeated wistfully. "Yeah, for sure."

Morgan pulled away. Emily stared at her for a moment with a confused smile. Morgan closed her eyes for a moment and took a deep breath. "Stop overthinking."

"What?" Emily giggled. Before she should say anything else, Morgan grabbed her face and kissed her on the lips.

At first it caught Emily completely off guard. It took a second to process what was happening. Should she pull away?

But her lips felt soft. She had that comforting Morgan smell of patchouli and lavender that Emily had begun to look forward to every morning. She could feel the curls of her friend's wild auburn hair dancing against her cheeks.

Emily decided not to freak out, or pull back dramatically. She just closed her eyes and went with it. Even kissed back. Nothing tawdry. Just a sweet, gentle extension of her own lips in return.

Emily had kissed a couple boys before, but nothing major. This felt different. It was, calming. She didn't entirely understand it, but she also didn't mind.

"I'm sorry," said Morgan, suddenly pulling her head back. "I shouldn't have done that."

"No," said Emily. "It's okay. Really. It's fine. I don't mind."

"I just . . . ," Morgan started. "You don't?"

"It was nice," said Emily.

"It was?"

"I mean, I didn't see it coming," said Emily. "But yeah, it was nice. I liked it."

"I don't expect anything," Morgan blurted out. "I just wanted you to know I care about you, and, . . . I, uh, . . . *damn it.* I have so many thoughts going on in my brain right now."

"You don't have to freak out about it," said Emily. "You can tell me whatever you need to when your brain settles down. It's just a kiss, right? You don't need to profess anything, or explain anything."

"Have you ever, you know, thought about things like that, before?" said Morgan. "With me, I mean. Or, any girl. We've never really talked about that kind of stuff. The boy-girl stuff, I mean."

"I don't know," Emily said, thinking about it. "Honestly, I've hung out with a few guys before, but nothing major. I've never had a boyfriend. And that was before I first changed. Since then, I haven't really thought about any of that stuff. Boys, girls, whatever. It's been hard to get close to anyone, let alone fall in love or whatever."

"Yeah, I get that," said Morgan. "I just hope this doesn't change anything. I really love you as a friend Em. I just want to be with you, as a friend, regardless of anything else. But, I just want you to know, I'm not afraid of you either."

"I know," Emily said. She took Morgan's hand. "I appreciate it."

"Hey guys, you should probably come downstairs," said Sophie reappearing in the doorway. Her eyes immediately fell to their hands. "Uh, this is new. Did I miss something?"

"What's going on?" Emily asked, letting go of Morgan.

"Something crazy downstairs," she said. "Come with me, but *stay cool*."

They both followed her out, exchanging perplexed looks, and walked down the hall to the staircase.

Sophie paused and turned back to them. "But do not think for a second that I won't be asking about whatever just happened in there later."

B. Andrew Scott

Chapter 13

Sophie led the girls halfway down the grand staircase until they could see Luther's back, blocking the front door in the foyer.

"It's the cops," Sophie whispered back to them.

"The police?" Morgan said. "What do they want?"

"I'm not sure," she answered. "I think they said they want to search my house."

"Shouldn't you go find out?" Emily asked.

"I was hoping to let Luther deal with them first," Sophie said. "Sometimes just seeing him at the door makes people change their minds. Even cops."

"Sophie," Luther called back over his shoulder, as if on cue. "I think you should come down here and speak to these gentlemen."

"Guess not this time," said Morgan.

Sophie walked down the white carpeted stairs to the tile foyer floor. She pulled the door open all the way and there stood a uniformed Charleston police officer, with three more behind him on the porch steps.

The one at the door was Stanley Crumshaw. He was well known on Lune de Sang.

Crumshaw patrolled the island every night. The others, she didn't recognize. There were also two other men standing on the walkway in ties and jackets – detectives, she figured. One was a fit, middle-aged black man. Beside him stood a shorter, doughy white guy with messy hair and cheap tie.

"How can I help you Officer Crumshaw?" Sophie asked.

"Miss Broussard," said Crumshaw in a very flat, steady voice. "Sorry to bother you, but I'm afraid I need to take a look around your house."

"I'm sorry," she said. "Why is that?"

"We've received information that you might have evidence on the premises somehow related to the disappearance of Tate Billings," said Crumshaw, in the same monotone voice.

"What the hell is a Tate Billings?" Sophie laughed. "And why I would have evidence connected to one?"

"The young man who went missing recently," the black man walking up the steps over Crumshaw's shoulder answered. He too had a low, emotionless voice. He held up a clear plastic bag with a smart phone inside. "Can you explain how this ended up under some bushes in your yard?"

"Well first you'll have to explain what it is?" she said.

"It's Tate's cell phone," the man said. "Billings was spotted in front of your house the night he disappeared. We're told the two of you exchanged unkind words."

"Oh, *that* little shit?" Sophie said, defiantly. "Yeah, as a matter of fact he did pass my house the other night. But I don't remember him tossing his phone in my grass, so I don't know how it got there. Maybe he's just a dumb slab of meat who doesn't respect expensive phones, abuses animals, and gets himself lost."

"Sophie," Luther growled behind her. "Don't fuck with cops."

"No, in fact I'd also like to know who the good citizen is that was snooping around my house, as many do, and just *happened* to find that phone," Sophie went on.

"You know I can't tell you that ma'am," Crumshaw said.

"Well, they got it wrong," Sophie told him. "I didn't say a word to the kid. Even if he was totally cool hurling some nasty little comments about my ethnic background at me and saying I don't belong. You wouldn't know anything about that sort of behavior, would you officer?"

"Ma'am, please just let us come in and look around," said Crumshaw. "The sooner we come in, the sooner we can leave."

"No way Sophie," Morgan shouted, marching down the stairs to the foyer. Emily followed behind her. "Make them show you a search warrant."

"Girl, don't worry, ," said Sophie. "I've seen Law & Order too. They're not searching my shit."

"They've tried rummaging around my mom's shop when somebody called in a report we were dealing ecstasy last year," Morgan went on. "It was total bullshit and we called them on it."

"This doesn't concern you ladies," said Crumshaw.

"Unless, maybe it does," the detective added.

"Wait a minute," Emily said, sniffing the air. She stepped forward and looked past Sophie at the men outside.

Emily immediately recognized Detective Akuna. And she could have smell Detective Torrance and his cheap drugstore cologne from across the island. "Morgan, it's the two detectives that came to school."

Morgan looked past Luther's bulk to see Detectives Akuna and Torrance outside with the uniformed officers. Something was off about them. Especially Akuna. Even for a cop, he'd seemed cool and outgoing the other day. Now he almost seemed robotic.

Morgan closed her eyes and quickly scanned Crumshaw's brain. Then she did the same with the detectives. They were both thinking the same thoughts.

"Get inside the house." Actually it felt more like an order. And it sounded like a singular voice. *"That's them,"* Morgan heard. *"The witch and the wolf. Get inside and finish this."*

This was bad. These policemen were not acting on their own. Someone was inside their minds. And this whole cell phone story was clearly bullshit. They weren't there to ask questions, or even make arrests. This was a hunting party.

"Sophie," Morgan said, trying to remain calm, but feeling her hands trembling. "Emily. Both of you should step back. Oh, and Sophie, you need to cover your eyes."

"What?" asked Sophie. "Why?"

"Morgan, what's going on?" Emily added.

"That presence we've all been discussing," Morgan responded, squinting at the officers. "I think it's nearby. And it's sent friends."

Morgan threw her hands out in front of her. All the officers reached for their guns.

"Bidh gaoth agus solas a 'tuiteam orra mar chuan. Cuir air falbh iad," the young witch chanted. ***"Cuir air falbh iad!"***

There was a crack of thunder and a deafening rumble, like a freight train was about to come crashing through the living room. It was followed by a blast of wind, stronger than a hurricane, and a blinding white light that erupted from Morgan's body.

All six men were forcefully lifted off their feet and back into the air, flailing over Saint Charles Boulevard before they were dropped, tumbling hard onto the beach on the other side.

Morgan stopped the spell and with a flick of her wrist, the

front door slammed shut, and all the locks turned.

"They'll be back," she said, spinning around. Emily was staring in disbelief. Sophie was slowly sliding her hands away from her eyes with a pained look on her face. Even the usually stoic Luther removed his sunglasses to stare at her in astonishment.

"Can someone explain to me what the hell just happened?" Sophie asked. "You can't just hurl the cops across the street Morgan. This is bad."

"Those cops weren't acting on their own," Morgan explained. "I could hear it. Someone was in their heads, controlling them. And whoever it was knows about us. All three of us. It called me a witch, and Emily a wolf. I have to assume it knows what you are too. He told them to get us inside and finish something."

"Finish what?" Emily asked. "Kill us?"

"Well I'm pretty sure they weren't going to ask us to the policemen's ball," said Sophie. They both stared blankly. "Sorry, it's an old-timey reference. I'm really ancient, remember? I don't even know if it was really a thing. Anyway, what do we do?"

"I don't know," said Morgan. "How secure is this house?"

"It's pretty tight," said Luther, pulling an enormous chrome pistol from his belt. It looked like it could punch holes in a tank. "But it's not a fortress. They could try blasting their way in."

"I want to know who tried to set me up for killing Tate?" Sophie asked. "How did they get his phone?"

"I think we're about to find out," said Morgan, pulling back the side of a curtain. "But I'd bet it's the same guy who sent them."

The men were all staggering back across the road, a couple of them looking pretty hurt, bloodied and dragging twisted or broken limbs. Yet they looked determined. Most likely they had no choice.

And they had their guns drawn.

"Sophie, go hide in the pantry," said Luther. "They won't be able to get in there. It's solid steel."

"No," said Sophie defiantly. "I'm not hiding Luther. These assholes came to kill me. I'm going to find out why. Besides, I'm bullet proof. What about you, Moonlight?"

"I don't know," said Emily, worried. "Never tested it. But Morgan's not."

"Then you both stay in here," said Sophie. "I'm going to find out who's playing games with us."

"Just remember, they don't have a choice," said Morgan. "Someone's pulling their strings."

"Fine," said Sophie, her eyes illuminated red like stoplights. Fangs slowly appeared from her gum line, two long and two shorter along the top, and two along the bottom. "I won't kill anyone, if I don't have to. But I'll sure as hell cut the strings."

"I'm going with you," said Emily.

"You're what?" Morgan coughed.

"Morgan, I'm not letting her go out there alone," said Emily. "But I need you to help me. I can't change at will. At least, I've never tried, for obvious reasons. You're going to have to help me turn it on."

"Turn it on," said Morgan. "Emily that's crazy. Attacking police officers? This could go very bad. What if your cover's blown? Remember you've got a family to protect."

"Morgan, you're the one who was just saying that maybe we were brought together by some other power," said Emily. "It's time we find out if you're right, and why. Until we do, no one is safe. Including my family."

"Just because I helped you remember, it doesn't mean you can suddenly control the wolf now," Morgan said.

"I don't need to," said Emily. "I've got you and Sophie to help with that now. All I need to do is fight. If I get out of control, you can shut me down."

"Oh it's that easy now, is it?" Morgan roller her eyes.

They heard a pop outside immediately followed by a window shattering as the police officers outside opened fire on the Broussard mansion. Luther smashed out a window with his elbow and began returning their fire.

"This is fucking crazy," Morgan screamed. She put her palm on Emily's forehead. Her hand was shaking. She had tears in her eyes looking at her friend. "You damn well better be bulletproof!"

"Don't worry," Emily smiled, choking back her own fear. "I'll be okay."

"Let's go, you two," Sophie demanded.

"I don't know how to do this," Morgan said silently. She found herself back inside Emily's mind. "I might have an idea though."

"I trust you," Emily told her.

Morgan placed her hands on either side of the lighted stream of Emily's thoughts. *"Lorg do chrodh. Lorg do chreach. Lorg an fiadh-bheathach. Leig leam a leigeil às."*

"What did you say?" Emily asked. She could feel her body begin to shake. Her brain was vibrating.

"It's Gaelic," said Morgan. "The language of my ancestors. I'm calling to your anger. Telling your rage to be free. To find the wild animal, and let it loose."

Emily could feel the wolf waking up. For once, she wasn't afraid. Maybe it wouldn't let her drive, but at least it might let her navigate.

"Say it again."

"Lorg do chrodh," Morgan repeated. *"Lorg do chreach. Lorg an fiadh-bheathach. Leig leam a leigeil às."*

Emily's chest began to heave and convulse. It was working. It felt like something was trying to break loose from her stomach.

"Now this part is going to suck," said Morgan. Once again, she released all the visions of Emily's previous attacks. Followed lastly by Tate Billings taunting her in the lunchroom, and the memory of the detective interrogating her about him later. *"Lorg do chrodh. Lorg do chreach. Lorg an fiadh-bheathach. Leig leam a leigeil às."*

"Morgan," Emily growled softly. *"Get away from me."*

Morgan took a step back, lifting her hand off Emily's head. She watched her friend's eyes roll back like a great white shark about to attack.

Her arm muscles rippled under the skin. Her fingers swelled and sharp curved claws pushed their way up from under her normal fingernails, which shrunk back into her hands. Emily's face winced and contorted.

This process was not peaceful or easy. Her flesh would not miraculously evaporate or tear away to reveal a wolf form. This was a transformation on a cellular level that twisted and reshaped her musculature and bones. And it was painful.

Sharp flesh tearing canines slid out of her gums, forcing her human teeth to recede into the gums. Her eyes opened to reveal two black slits in pools of bright green.

She spoke in a horrible voice that was not her own. *"I said go!"*

Luther grabbed Morgan from behind and pulled her away, dragging her down the hall. They both watched in silent horror as the transformation completed.

Emily tore her clothing away. They could hear her bones separating, twisting, and rejoining in new alignments. Her muscles swelled. Her arms and legs stretched. Her thighs became rock solid machines to propel her body forward.

Finally, Emily's skull punched forward, turning her nose and mouth into an animalistic muzzle. Her pointed ears appeared from under her long black hair. Thick hair sprouted from every follicle on her skin, soon covering her body in a smooth dark coat. She scanned the room, sniffing the air.

Her eyes locked in on Morgan and Luther down the hallway and she let loose a low, guttural growl.

"*Emily*, no," Sophie barked, strong and commanding. "They're friends."

Her head snapped to see the vampire hovering above the ground a few feet away, eyes blazing, fangs bared.

Emily made a savage, snarling sound.

"I don't know if she's in there," Morgan muttered, afraid she might attack Sophie again. "She needs me."

"Are you crazy?" Luther said, tightening his grip on her. "Your friend's not home at the moment. That thing is a wild animal and will rip you to shreds. Sophie can handle it."

"*Scaoileadh!*" Morgan commanded. It was the Gaelic word for *release*, and Luther's gorilla arms did just that. He let go of her against his will as his arms flew up over his head.

Morgan ran towards Emily who was rearing back, ready to strike at Sophie. "Emily, I know you're in there. Take back control."

"Morgan, get out of here," Sophie shouted from across the room. She wasn't sure if she should attack the puppet police officers or save her little witch friend from their werewolf friend.

Without warning, Emily leapt toward Morgan, jaws opened to strike her throat and take her down like prey.

"Decision made," Sophie muttered, rushing at Emily, and tackling her from the side. The two mythic creatures tumbled across the floor. They rolled into a wall, smashing a cabinet of antique vases.

Morgan was terrified. She feared they would kill each other, or that Emily would break away and kill her. It didn't matter. That was still her friend. She ran towards them as they wrestled - Sophie trying to subdue her, while Emily's jaws snapped open and shut, possessed by the instinct to kill.

"Can you grab her mouth?" Morgan asked. "I need to touch her forehead."

"What am I?" Sophie grunted as she struggled. "A gator wrestler? I'll try."

She knew in these forms, Emily was much stronger than her, and it would only be seconds before she threw Sophie off like a ragdoll. She reached for Emily's snout. She was too slow.

White fangs ripped into her brown arm. "*Goddammit!*"

Morgan screamed when she saw blood spray from Sophie's arm. "Are you okay?"

"Yeah, I'm super awesome," Sophie winced. "I'm a vampire. I'll heal. It just . . . fucking . . . hurts!"

Pissed off, Sophie reached out quickly, grabbed Emily's snout, and slammed her teeth together.

Morgan didn't hesitate. She fell to her knees and pressed her hand against Emily's furry brow. Emily's mind was no longer the calm tunnel of many colored lights. It was a maelstrom of burning red. Everything was shaking like a Magnitude 5 earthquake with the lights and sounds of a 5-alarm fire.

"Emily, stop this," she ordered. "Stop this attack now. We are your friends. **Stop this now!**"

The wolf stopped struggling. Her muscles loosened and she quit flailing her head back and forth. Sophie slowly moved her hands away.

"Subdue this monster in you," Morgan went on, whispering petitions for peace. "Take control. *Smacht a fháil ar an ainmhí seo!* Take control. Use your power to help us, and to help yourself."

Morgan opened her eyes for a moment. Emily's were closed. She was breathing calmly, as if being soothed.

"Great Cerridwen, Goddess of transformation, give this sweet spirit control of her gift. Goddess Hecate, give her power over it. Goddess Luna, comfort your child."

The werewolf opened its eyes. They blazed like emeralds, but Morgan was somehow certain she no longer saw murder in their reflection. She took her hand away from Emily's head.

"Emily," she said softly. "Are you there? Can you hear me now?"

The creature stared at her a moment without moving. Sophie stood poised for attack, in case things went bad. If Emily attacked Morgan now, it would be very hard to get to her in time. Slowly, Emily nodded her head up and down.

"You can?" Morgan asked. She began to cry and laugh. "You can hear me? Are you in control?"

After a moment, Emily reared back and slowly stood on her hind legs. Her arms hung out at her sides, claws bared. She turned her head from Morgan to Sophie and back to Morgan. Again she nodded.

She was there. She was the wolf, but she was also Emily. She'd never been this lucid in this body. It was overwhelming. But she seemed to have control.

"Umm, this is a really great moment and everything," said Sophie, "but we have six brainwashed cops on the porch about to blast the door down. Emily, you up for a fight? Let's do this."

Emily's lips peeled back and to reveal a row of deadly crescent teeth as she growled her approval and turned to face the front door.

"Luther," Sophie said, "take Morgan and get out of here. Go

to the pantry."

"I'm not letting you two go out there alone," said Morgan.

"I'm sorry," said Sophie. She nodded at Luther, who wrapped a massive arm around Morgan. "Everyone who isn't immortal, or just crazy, strong and clawed, please stop arguing with me.

Morgan, you've done your part. And we appreciate it. But get out of here. We've got this."

"Open the door, bitch," one of the cops called from the porch as he banged on the door with his gun.

"*Bitch?*" Sophie repeated, eyes wide. "I was *ma'am* a few minutes ago. Now I'm bitch? Emily, get ready. I am going to open that door."

Sophie rushed at the door and kicked it hard, sending it swinging out and smacking Crumshaw in the face. His nose exploded into bloody goo as he fell backwards into the two detectives. All three landed on their backs. The other officers began firing their pistols.

"Emily," Sophie called out. "Remember that whole *no killing* thing? Forget it. Let's eat."

The black she-wolf gave an approving bark and leapt through the open door, smelling Crumshaw's fresh blood. She landed hard on his chest, breaking his ribs, and bit down into his soft flabby throat, tearing the meat from the bone.

Detective Akuna was pinned underneath them. His eyes were opaque and his face showed no emotion as his body struggled to get loose. Emily slashed at his face with her claws, ripping through his lips, nose, and one of his eyes.

"This is bad," Luther grunted, still watching from the entryway. His protective grip around Morgan loosened a bit. "The whole neighborhood's going to see this."

"Maybe not," Morgan said. "If you let me go, I can help."

He made a thoughtful grunt, as if mulling it over.

"From inside the house," she added, annoyed.

"Fine," he said, letting her go.

Morgan stepped to the open doorway. She closed her eyes and raised her hands. "Okay, let's see if I can do this one."

"Bidh màthraichean spiorad gràsmhor a 'tarraing nan deòir a chaill thu airson uimhir de nigheanan a thuit bhon ùir agus a' dìon mo pheathraichean," she called out. "Thoir uisge às an talamh, gu sùilean dall dall mun cuairt."

"What the hell was all that?" Luther asked.

"Gaelic," she answered.

"Yeah but what did you say?"

"If I did it right," she said, opening her eyes, "you're about to see."

A white mist began to rise from the wet grass, but strangely only on the edges of the yard. The fog thickened as it rose and danced through the air. It wasn't long until walls of milky condensation surrounded the entire mansion. It hung on the air, showing no signs of dissipating any time soon.

"That will do," Luther said.

Unfazed by the mist, Sophie hurled herself at the three uniformed officers, not even feeling their bullets. She grabbed two of them by the neck, sinking her nails into their flesh and hoisted them into the air. She threw them down hard against the street.

The third continued to fire on her, but his shots barely stung. Sophie lunged at the cop, throwing his firing hand backward, hyper-extending his elbow and savoring the crack as the bone split and tore through the blue sleeve of his uniform. He made no sound to signify pain. This poor cop wasn't even present in his own body.

His face was completely expressionless. Whatever, Sophie thought. He still had blood coursing through his veins. She bit down into his shoulder. Whatever spell had been cast over him must have broken in that moment, because the policeman began to scream bloody murder.

"Quiet you baby," Sophie sneered through precious sips, reaching out and twisting his head by the jaw until it snapped. His body went limp and she pulled her fangs from his flesh. She spat a bloody wad on his chest.

"Your blood tastes like rust," she sneered. "Would it have hurt you to drink a little juice now and then."

"Get offa him now," Sophie heard a man yell behind her.

She turned to see the chubby Detective Torrance with his pistol drawn on Emily who had not a care in the world. She had thrown Crumshaw aside and was now tearing into Detective Akuna's chest, looking for that sweet heart meat.

With trembling hands, Torrance fired four shots into Emily's side at point blank range. She fell sideways off Akuna's body with a yelp.

"*Emily*," Sophie cried.

The vampire charged through the air and snatched Torrance by his sweaty, curly hair. She smashed his face through what glass was left in one of the windows they'd shot up. She pulled him back, his face cut up and bleeding in a hundred places. She ran her tongue up the side of his cheek, lapping up the streaming blood.

"Now you, I like," she said, with a tinge of playful flirtation.

"You've got a real sweet tooth, don't you?"

Torrance begged for his life, but Sophie wasn't interested. She opened her jaws wide and buried her teeth into his jugular, draining him of as much life-giving fluid as his panicked heart could pump her way.

When she'd had her fill, Sophie dropped his limp body. Sophie wiped her mouth with the back of her hand, smearing blood across her lips and cheek. She was satiated, at least for the moment.

Down in the street, the last two cops had managed to get to their feet, bewildered and pained, as whatever trance they were under had been broken. One looked up and locked eyes with Sophie, accessing her standing over bodies on the porch.

"What the hell?" he yelled. He lifted his gun with a shaky hand and began firing. Not a single shot came close to landing. It wouldn't have mattered if they had.

"Great," Sophie rolled her eyes. "I'm not even hungry anymore. But, I guess I can make room."

She didn't even have a chance to attack. A slobbering black blur flew past her shoulder, bounding down the steps toward the policemen.

Without slowing down, Emily leapt sideways in the air, landed on one of the officers, locking her jaws around his neck and twisting her whole body around, flipping him. It was an astonishing, primal attack meant to immediately incapacitate the victim.

They both hit the ground and she violently shook her head like a dog, just emerged from a swimming pool. His blood sprayed all over the asphalt. With one last yank of her jaw, she tore his head clean from his body.

"Holy shit," said Sophie. "She is bullet proof."

Sophie jumped the deck rail and flew over the lawn to the street where the last cop stood frozen with terror. He just held his pistol limp at his side.

His lips moved, trying to find words, but nothing came out. He was probably telling himself this was a bad dream. Maybe he'd had too much to drink and was sleeping it off safe in his bed.

"Who told you to come here?" Sophie wrapped her fingers around his throat.

"I – I . . . don't," he stammered. "What are you?"

"Answer my question," she demanded, tightening her grip. "Who told you to come to my home, and kill us? Tell me now, or you can be dessert."

"I swear, I don't know," he said. "He never said his name."

"I'll find out," Morgan said, coming down the steps from the house. She looked around at the remains of their assailants. Emily had her jaws around the top of her victim's skull.

"I'm actually impressed you two left one to question," Morgan added.

"Well, you know," Sophie shrugged with a smile. "Cosmo says it's good to push away while you still have a little left on your plate. Emily's just playing with her food over there. Seriously, we really need to teach the girl some manners."

Morgan pushed past the vampire and slapped her hand on the officer's forehead. The young witch closed her eyes and seemingly transferred her consciousness into the man's mind.

After a few moments, Morgan opened her eyes and took her hand off his head. She stared at Sophie in disbelief.

"You're not going to believe this," Morgan told Sophie. "It's the guy from the bus stops. The real estate guy."

"*Griess?*" Sophie asked. "What? He was just here for dinner a few weeks ago. He's a slimy salesman, but he's not a monster."

"Apparently he's both," she said. "And he wants all three of us dead."

"Why? What did we do to him?"

"Don't know," Morgan shrugged. "He didn't tell these guys. Just sent them to try to kill us. Or draw us out, I'm not sure."

"Fuck," said Sophie. "So he purposely sent them to be slaughtered."

"More or less," said Morgan.

"And we fell for it," Sophie said. "Damn it. I've spent decades trying to stay under the radar. In one night, I litter my lawn with dead bodies. This is definitely not low-key!"

"What do we do with this?" asked Morgan, pointing her thumb at the petrified police officer.

"I'm really not hungry anymore," said Sophie. "And it feels wrong to just kill him now. But we can't risk having him out there either."

"Look at him," said Luther, appearing on the porch steps. "He's a mess. He's not a threat to you."

"Luther's right," said Morgan. "I've seen inside his thoughts. His brain is scrambled right now. Probably won't remember anything about tonight."

"Fine," said Sophie. "Let him go, I guess."

Morgan placed her hand on his forehead again and closer her eyes. "Run," she whispered.

The officer did exactly an instructed. He took off running

without looking back. Within a few seconds he vanished through the fog and was long gone.

"I'll take care of this mess," Luther said, standing on the porch. "You two need to grab wolf girl and get lost for a while."

"I'm not hiding from some cheesy realtor," said Sophie.

"Then what do you suggest we do?" Morgan asked.

Sophie looked over to Emily who was now back up on her hind legs watching them both, blood matted in her fur.

"I say we go find out what this dickhead's problem is," Sophie answered.

Chapter 14

Sophie and Morgan beckoned Emily to follow them. She took an unsure step, then fell in a heap to the street. The black hair covering her body began to recede back into her skin.

Her animal snout tightened back up until her face was once again that of a young woman, with a human mouth and nose. Her limbs contorted back into their normal positions and her muscles constricted and shrunk like deflating balloons.

Emily laid there, naked, shivering, and completely unconscious in the middle of the street.

"Damn," said Morgan, running over to her. "We have to get her inside."

"Was it the margaritas?" Sophie quipped, following her.

"The change just takes so much out of her," Morgan explained. "Her dad told me this happens every time. That's why he follows her out, to scoop her up and gets her back into bed before anyone finds her."

"What are we supposed to do?" Sophie asked. "Griess is out there. If he realizes we know it's him, he may do something desperate. I want to get to him first."

"We can't leave her like this," Morgan snapped. "Help me get her into the house."

"Fine, you're right," said Sophie. Her eyes returned to their normal hazel and her fangs slid back into her skull. "But damn it, if Griess runs for it I'm going to be pissed."

The two of them propped Emily's arms over their shoulders and carried her limp body into the house. Sophie could have easily managed, but Morgan didn't want to let go of her. They laid Emily on the sofa with a blanket draped over her.

"Do you think you have any clothes she can wear?" Morgan asked.

"Probably," said Sophie. "Might be a little tall for her but I'll figure something out." Sophie ran up the stairs to her room.

Morgan dug around in her bag. She found a small vile of oil. She dabbed a few drops onto her fingers and rubbed them together before waving them Emily's nose. The aroma was potent – citrus, eucalyptus, and other strong herbs. Morgan placed a gentle hand on her friend's head and waved her fingers under her nose.

"Emily," she spoke. "Can you wake up?"

After a second, Emily took a deep breath through her nose and her eyelids fluttered open. There was a brief moment of panic on her face as she didn't recognize where she was, until she saw Morgan. She took a deep breath and let her head fall back gently.

"What happened?" she asked. Then she closed her eyes again and sighed.

"You don't have to tell me," she said quietly. "I remember. Most of it, I think, anyway."

"Yeah, those cops aren't really an issue anymore," Morgan said, stroking her hair. "If it helps, you guys didn't kill all of them. This whole situation is screwed up."

"Where's Sophie?" Emily asked.

"Upstairs, finding you something to wear," Morgan said. "You kind of shredded your clothes."

"Yup," Emily nodded. "That happens."

"And we know who sent the cops after us," Morgan said. "It was Amman Griess."

"Wait," Emily squinted, thinking. "The real estate guy?"

"Yes," Morgan nodded.

"Why is a realtor trying to kill us?" she asked. "And what, is he a psychic or something?"

"That I don't know," Morgan said. "But I definitely saw him in one of the officer's head."

"Here, these might fit," said Sophie reappearing with clothes in her arms. She set them on Emily's chest. "The pants are a little short for me so they should work for you. Probably better if you actually had an ass."

"Are you serious?" Emily asked, holding up a pair of dark red leather pants.

"Girl, this isn't Macy's," Sophie shrugged. "How are you feeling?"

"Woozy," Emily said, pinching the bridge of her nose. "This is new. I don't know if it's from wolfing out, or the margaritas."

"You'll get used to . . . well, at least one of those for sure," Sophie smiled. "I'm going after Griess. I can take Luther with me. You two can stay if you're not up to it. It's okay."

"Maybe we should wait," Morgan said.

"For what?" Sophie asked. "To give him time to disappear? Or worse, regroup? He could send an entire army next time. Or he could just come after us one at a time. Emily has a family. Morgan, you have your mom. We need to confront Griess before he comes for us again."

"She's right," Emily said, swinging her legs around and putting her feet on the wood floor. She steadied herself, feeling a bit dizzy. "You heard what he told those cops. He wants us dead. I'm not waiting for him to grab my mom and dad, or my little brother."

"We might need wolf-Emily again," said Morgan, worried. "Are you sure you can handle it again, so soon?"

"She makes a point," said Sophie. "Have you ever done it twice in a night before?"

"It doesn't matter," said Emily. "I have to now." She paused and forced a smile. "I'll probably tear up these leather pants though."

"Emily, this is serious," said Morgan sternly. "You could be putting yourself at risk."

Emily stood up. "I'm not afraid Morgan. You'll be there to help me."

The two just shared a gaze, neither speaking for a moment.

"Um, are you two about to do something?" Sophie finally asked. "Normally I'd be all about that, but we need to go."

"Shut up Sophie," they both said in unison. Emily pulled the black tee over her body. Then she squeezed into the leather pants.

"I look like I work at Coyote Ugly," said Emily, looking in a floor length mirror in the entryway.

"Do you need shoes?" Sophie asked. "Because I'm not sure if I have anything that your canoes could squeeze into."

"Why should I bother with shoes?" Emily asked. "My feet will be paws soon anyway, right?"

The terrified police officer ran for his life. He cut between houses, hopping over fences, and sprinting through yards, never looking back. His head was throbbing. He wasn't sure what had just happened. He just knew he needed to get away, whatever it took.

He darted out around the corner of a two story mansion on Flor De Lis Avenue. A stranger stepped out of the shadows in front of him. It startled the cop and he fell to the damp grass. It took a moment to recognize the man as Amman Griess.

The officer only knew the man from his advertisements around town, but he felt familiar with him. Obligated even, as if there was something he was supposed to do for the man, but he couldn't remember what or why. His ears were ringing.

"Well, what happened?" Griess asked.

"What? What do you mean?"

"Did you kill the witch?"

"Say what?" he asked, confused. "What are talking about? What witch?"

"The bookish girl with the curly hair and glasses," hissed Griess. "Did you shoot her as I told you to do?"

The policeman had no clue what this man was talking about. What girl? Why would he shoot someone?

"I . . . I don't understand," the officer stammered. "Shoot who? We were at the Broussard house, and we were attacked. Some kind of big animal. A dog maybe. I don't know. I feel like I'm having a nervous breakdown. I can't think, man. Nothing is clear right now."

"That's because your mind is feeble," Griess rolled his eyes. "Between all your screens and your mobile devices, modern humanity is doomed. It's the reason for my resurrection."

Griess stepped closer to the cop. He placed a caring hand on his shoulder and squeeze gently. The officers eyes were glassy and frightened.

"It's not your fault," Griess said softly. "Don't worry. You have nothing to be afraid of anymore. I've been brought back to bring order to everything. There will be a difficult time of adjustment, of course. That's unavoidable. Change, and growth, must be accompanied with pain. But don't let that bother you. You won't be here to experience it."

The bewildered policeman watched as the face of Amman Griess began to wrinkle and discolor. His lips rolled back, revealing graying gums and rotting, yellow teeth. His eyes became gooey and green like moss. A rank odor assaulted the officer's nostrils. It was the smell of death and decay.

He'd experienced a similar scent once before, when he'd entered an apartment to find a deceased resident no one had checked on in weeks. It was the worst thing he'd ever smelled in his life. Until now.

Griess' jaw unhinged and hung low, as his mouth began to make a horrible sucking sound like a broken vacuum. The helpless officer felt a strange sensation pulling at his face. The pressure increased in intensity. His eyeballs felt like they were being sucked out of his skull. He couldn't breathe.

The pressure was unbearable. He wanted to scream, but couldn't draw the breath to do it. Darkness began creeping in from the corners of his eyes. The last thing the cop saw was a strange iridescent fog billowing out of his own mouth and the horrific image of Amman Griess sucking in his life force.

A moment later, the police officer's lifeless body dropped to the ground in a heap. Griess touched his fingers to his own face, feeling how the flesh was again soft and fresh.

Feeding off the other man's soul had replenished his own body. But it was, as always, only to be a temporary solution. There was just one thing that would make him completely whole, and better.

He needed to get back to his house quickly, and prepare to claim it.

Chapter 15

Amman Griess lived in a white revival style mansion two blocks away, with a cupola at the top that used to boast a cross.

The house was completely restored. There were two beautiful magnolia trees in the front yard. The landscaping was meticulous, and the grass well-manicured. Griess seemed as vein about his home as he was about his own personal appearance.

But, they all agreed it was surprising someone as polished as Griess would choose a home that was rumored to sit on a secret cemetery.

All the windows were shuttered and dark when the three girls arrived at the front gate.

"Do you think he took off?" Emily wondered as they stared up at the house.

"No," said Sophie. "He's here. I can just sense it."

"And I'd bet he knows we are too," Morgan added.

"Then he's being very rude," said Sophie. "Invite us in, asshole. I'm not going to hover at the gate." With that she kicked the gate in and stomped up the brick walk to the door.

"If he didn't know we were here, he does now," Emily said.

Morgan looked at Emily, concerned. "Are you sure you're good?"

"Yes," Emily said, waving off her concern. "Come on. There's three of us. There's only one of him, right?"

"Who knows?" Morgan shrugged.

"What are the odds he has another werewolf, vampire, and witch in there?" Emily joked. "For all we know, he's just some carnie con man that knows how to hypnotize cops."

"I do love carnies," Morgan smiled.

Emily started to follow Sophie up the path.

"Just in case," she said, stopping and turning back. "Earlier tonight, at Sophie's, "you know, when it was just us. I just wanted to say, that was nice."

Morgan was immediately grateful that the magnolia over her head was blocking the moonlight, as she knew of no spell that would disguise the fact that she was blushing.

"Yeah," she started, her voice cracking. "I thought so too."

"I just felt like I should say it," said Emily. "Just in case, well, you know. I'm not sure what it means, but . . .."

"Emily, it's okay," said Morgan. "We're sixteen. We don't need to have everything figured out yet."

"Will you two come on?" Sophie barked. She was already on the porch. She banged her fist on the red front door. "Open the door, Griess!"

No lights came on in the house. The lock on the door did not click. Sophie rolled her eyes. She took a step back, then lunged forward, pushing her shoulder into the door. The bolts smashed through the frame, launching splinters of wood everywhere as it swung open.

Sophie walked brazenly into the foyer without hesitation and flipped up the first few light switches along the wall. The hall and adjacent parlor lit up. The other girls followed her inside.

"What in the actual . . . ?" Sophie mumbled, looking around. "Were we just transported to Trump Tower?"

There was a study on the right and a dining room on the left, and both were staged with the gaudiest gold furniture and finishing's any of them had ever seen. There were golden statues of cherubs and birds.

The dining room table was marble and set with gold plates and cutlery for ten. The chairs were painted in gold. There was a bar in the corner with gold finishes and bottles of expensive wines filled a rack. A gold platter was piled high with grapes and figs.

In the parlor, more gold adorned chairs and a white sofa. The carpet was a thick white plush. There were tall statues of gold and black onyx standing in each corner of the room. One with a man's body and a dog-like head. Another with the head of a bird.

"Those are Egyptian, right?" Emily asked.

"Yep," Morgan answered. "That's Anubis, the jackal-headed god of the dead. Horus, the falcon god of the sky. The other bird guy is probably his dad, Ra, the sun god. He was the Egyptians' main deity." She pointed at the fourth, a particularly weird one. "That guy over there that looks a bit like an anteater is Seth. He's particularly nasty. The god of violence, and pain."

"Just the guy you'd keep in your house to greet guests," said Sophie.

They all crept further down the hall toward the back of the house. It opened up into a large kitchen which was also dark. When she switched on the light, the room was spotless and organized. It didn't look as though anyone had actually used this kitchen for cooking in a long time. In fact, it looked like it had been staged by a realtor.

"Uh, guys," Emily said from the adjacent room across the hall. "Check this out."

In what would have normally been a living room, maybe with a loveseat and television where a family would hang out, there were no furnishings at all. Instead there were only stacks and stacks of shiny bricks. Solid gold bricks.

"What the hell?" Sophie whispered.

"The robberies," said Emily.

"Robberies?" said Sophie.

"I heard about it on tv the other morning," Emily explained, examining the gold bars. "Two armored trucks carrying gold from New York to Fort Knox have been hit in the last couple weeks. Both of them happened within a few hours of here."

"You think Griess is robbing armored cars?" Morgan said. "That doesn't make sense."

"Like any of this makes sense," Emily offered, holding her hands up. "Me, Sophie, the telepathic real estate guy. Seems like anything's possible now."

"So, he's psychic *and* he hijacks armored cars like he's in the *Fast & The Furious?*" Sophie quipped.

"I mean," Emily gestured at the evidence gleaming before them. "It's right here."

"But why would a guy like Griess risk the rest of his life in prison?" asked Morgan. "And even if he did, how would he get in here without getting caught?"

"Not to mention," Sophie added, "good luck trying to unload it for cash without getting caught."

"I have no intention of redeeming it for cash," said a man's voice all three of them knew in the hallway behind them.

All three girls screamed and spun around, fists clenched for a fight.

There stood Amman Griess. His fingers were adorned in his usual gold rings, and shiny bracelets encircled his wrists, but he was not wearing one of his signature three-piece suits.

Instead, Griess wore a white cloth around his waist, secured by a golden fiber belt. Aside from that, he was practically naked.

His chest was surprisingly muscular, and he had a number of white scars over his left pectoral muscle. His hair was slicked back tight across his head. Black eyeliner encircled his eyes, which looked dilated and disturbed.

Inside the belt was tucked the ornate curved dagger with the Ankh handle. At his other side was a small leather whip.

All three girls exchanged concerned looks. Why was he standing there almost nude? They didn't think he'd be stupid enough to try to rape or assault them. He obviously knew what they were, and that he'd have zero chance against them alone.

"Hello ladies," he said. "Welcome to my home."

"Just out of the shower, are we Griess?" Sophie said with a sneer.

"I'll be getting dressed soon," he answered. "I heard you rummaging around down here in my home and thought it would be rude not to say hello. Although I must tell you, I'm disappointed, although not surprised to see all three of you here."

"After you tried to have us killed, you mean," Morgan said.

"Oh right," Sophie added. "I knew we came by for a reason. Pro-tip, dumb shit, bullets don't work on Emily, or me."

"Shooting Miss Morrison was never the plan," Griess said calmly. "That, I assume, was the panicked act of a scared police officer. If I'd wanted the dog dead, I'd have armed them with silver bullets. I only ordered the inept police officers to kill the witch."

"Me?" Morgan said. "What did I do to you? I don't even know you."

"You interfered," Griess answered. "You inserted yourself where you didn't belong. For years I've been bowing and scraping before the bloated, pasty, rich citizens of this island. I sat at their tables and forced myself to smile over their paltry excuses for feasts. All the while wanting to kill them, or myself, in order to escape this Hell."

"Then why didn't you?" Emily asked.

"Yeah, you could've saved us the trouble," Sophie added.

"You little girls just don't understand," Griess continued. "I wasn't born into this life. I was never meant to sell pathetic clapboard mansions to the undeserving wealthy of America. I was supposed to be a king."

Griess paused, seeing the confusion in their faces. He chuckled and nodded. "Oh, it only gets stranger," he said. "In fact, I was born to be a living god."

Sophie caught Emily's eyes and put her fingers to her lips to imply perhaps he'd been smoking something. Morgan, listening and watching him intently, elbowed her.

"Yes, it sounds crazy, but it's true," Griess went on. "You

see, I was born in the year your people call 1480 **BC**. My mother's name was Queen *Hatshepsut*."

"Hatshepsut?" Morgan repeated. "The female Pharaoh?"

"Very good young witch," Griess nodded. "I see you are well-read. Although my mother was actually the second woman to rule as Pharaoh."

"Hatshepsut was hailed as an amazing leader," said Morgan. "She was one of the most prolific builders of the Egyptian world."

"It's true," said Griess. "And she was hated for it. My mother had many enemies, simply because she was a woman. They smiled and bowed in her presence, but plotted in the shadows."

"I didn't even know there were women Pharaohs," Emily said.

"They aren't taught in many Western history books," said Morgan. "I learned of her in a women's studies course. She was very powerful. But there's a problem. The story already doesn't add up because most accounts say Hatshepsut was, well, ..."

"Gay?" Griess laughed. "Mother didn't like labels, but yes, before I was born she loved men and women. It's sad to think that in some ways the world was more tolerant about sex three-thousand years ago than it is now. But there you have it. My mother was shrewd, and married my father to keep her throne."

"I've read she fell in love with a woman," said Morgan, "but was forced to marry her own brother, or be put to death."

"Wait, your dad is your uncle?" Sophie asked.

"Quiet, demon," he snapped. "Don't speak of my family. Yes, he married her, to save her, and let her continue to rule. It was a different time. There was no one else worthy. My blood is royal."

"Even if we believed any of this," said Emily. "How come we never learned about a Pharaoh Griess in History class?" She looked to Morgan. "We didn't, right?"

"No," Morgan shook her head.

"Because I was betrayed before I could ascend to the throne," Griess explained. "By my own brother. My mother's bastard child that she bore before me with her falconer. They became very close, as my mother loved to join him on the hunt. My brother was the result. They hid him in the falconer's quarters, and my mother would see him in secret."

"Until she decided to reveal who he was, and make a declaration that he would succeed her as Pharaoh. My father was rightly enraged. He had the falconer beheaded on the spot. The next day, my half-brother bribed a trio of treacherous palace guards to stab me seven times as I slept. That's where these came from."

Griess rubbed a hand over the scars in his chest. They were certainly convincing.

"Yet here you stand," challenged Sophie.

"Says the 200-year-old vampire standing beside a werewolf," Morgan muttered back. "Still, there certainly are a lot of holes in your story. What's your real name? The one your family gave you?"

"I was born Prince Thutmose, the Third," he said. "Named after my father, and his father before him. I adopted the name Amman Griess at the suggestion of the Egyptian family who took me in."

"How did you end up in South Carolina?" Emily asked.

"Clearly I don't know many details," he said. "I was embalmed and wrapped, in the ancient tradition of my people. But my treacherous brother, the new Pharaoh, demanded my sarcophagus be unmarked. It was his final insult, to ensure no one would know who it held."

"This is like a Nicholas Cage movie," Sophie muttered under her breath to Emily.

"I awoke, roughly twenty years ago, in a museum restoration room," Griess continued. "As if I'd only been in a deep sleep. I had no idea how many millennia had passed. But my decrepit body showed it. My skin was gray and dry. My muscles had completely atrophied. I was so cold I couldn't stop shaking. But whoever had restored me was nowhere to be seen."

"Mummies don't just wake up after three-thousand years," said Morgan.

"My only clue was this," Griess said, holding out the ankh dagger. "It was lying at my feet. I knew it well. Every

Egyptian child of royalty knew of this dagger. It belonged to a sorcerer in the first Pharaoh's court."

"This is crazy," said Emily. She pointed her finger from Morgan to Emily, then back to herself. "Witch. Werewolf. Vampire. And now a *mummy*?"

"If there's a scaly green fish guy swimming around the coast of Lune de Sang, I'm done," cracked Sophie.

"You joke too much *blood sucker*," Griess said. His eyes glared at her. "This is a dark universe. But you will not be laughing much longer."

"Tut-tut, Tut," she said, rolling her eyes. "You may be older than me, but I've been awake a hell of a lot longer. You'll learn in time, it's the only way to survive in this world."

"But you have no idea who woke you up?" Morgan asked.

"I've spent decades trying to figure out that mystery," he said. "My sarcophagus was part of a traveling exhibit. When I woke in that New York museum, it was dark and empty. It took every ounce of strength I could muster to tear free of my wrappings." Griess mimed breaking free of his ceremonial bonds.

"I crawled out of the museum after feeding on the slower rats scurrying throughout the museum's basement," he said. "And then there was a night watchman I discovered sleeping at his post. I felt no remorse. The penalty for a sleeping palace guard was to be locked in a box with flesh eating beetles. I merely drank his lifeforce. And it did much to replenish my strength. I ran as best I could, in the guards ill-fitting pants, for many city blocks. I had no idea where I was. I'd never seen electric lights, let alone skyscrapers, or automobiles."

"I can't imagine," Emily said softly.

"Jesus, Emily," Sophie snapped. "Don't start sympathizing with the psychotic mummy guy."

"I found a small community of Egyptian immigrants in the city," Griess explained. "They helped me learn the language, and obtain a new identity. It took a great deal of adjusting, but after a time, I accepted my fate, and my new world. Eventually I enrolled at the local college. I studied real estate because the city's giant architecture fascinated me. I set sales records my first year in the profession. I'd love to tell you it was all based on my charm, but the truth is, this little item helped me with that."

He rolled the dagger around in his hand.

"Along with the power to wake the dead, whoever holds this dagger wields great powers of influence," he went on. "It was amazing. Every client bought the first house I showed them. And every seller accepted my first offer."

"You possess a phenomenal supernatural artifact," said Morgan, "and you used it for a real estate scam."

"I needed something they call *start-up capital*," Griess retorted. "I was not going to be a pauper in this world. And I wanted to explore, beyond New York. Eventually I stumbled across South Carolina and Lune de Sang. Something about this island drew me in. There's a lot of blood in the soil."

"I'm sick of this story, " Emily demanded. "What does this have to do with us?"

"Nothing," Griess answered. "And yet, perhaps everything. At first, I thought I could be satisfied with being alive, having amassed a small fortune. I could blend in with island society, and perhaps even let go of the anger and confusion that had consumed me from the moment I was awakened. I tried so hard to forgive my brother's betrayal, even as I still leapt awake so many nights, feeling phantom blades piercing my chest. And then a year ago I was given a sign."

He pointed at Sophie. "It was you. On a late-night walk, I saw you - the *real* you, feeding on an innocent man in Heron's Landing."

"Me?" Sophie said, incredulously. "I never . . . .." She paused, thinking back. "Oh, right. Dang it. There was that little slip-up. But for the record, he wasn't innocent. He was a bar trolling asshole with a pocket full of *rufies* and duct tape in his car."

"*Quiet*," Griess roared. "In that moment I was shown what I had to do to fulfill the will of the gods and ignite my own destiny."

"I'm sorry, I must have missed it," said Emily. "What is that destiny, and what does it have to do with Sophie, or any of us?"

"I was resurrected to reclaim my birthright," Griess said. "I must rebuild my family's dynasty. But I need her blood to do it." He glared at Sophie.

"Alright then," said Sophie pushing past the other two. "Now we get down to it. You want me? I'm right here. You want blood? Come take it."

"Sophie stop," said Emily grabbing for her arm.

"Stupid girl," said Griess. "I would never demean myself by touching you. I know I cannot kill you. My mind is powerful, as a king's should be, but my body is still no match for your demonic power. But by your supernatural blood, I will awaken my divine power. I too will become immortal.

"You want to be immortal?" said Emily.

"Of course," said Griess. "The Pharaohs were gods on earth. But not even they could conquer the grave. With Ra's Dagger and the power of her blood, I will live forever. And I will raise an army of the dead to subdue this world, castigate and depose your failed governments, and create the one world order that the gods demand. *The new Egypt.*"

Griess walked behind the kitchen counter and bent down, opening a cabinet. All three girls immediately became defensive. Sophie felt her fangs begin to slide out of hiding. He straightened up, holding a big white box, which he set on the counter.

"However, to attain that kind of power, I must spill the demon's blood. For that, I require a proper weapon. And I found it."

"What weapon?" Emily asked.

"It's in a hat box?" Sophie added.

"The perfect machine built to hunt and kill her kind," Griess answered with a sardonic grin, staring Emily right in the eyes. "The kind that is predisposed to hate vampires. The one whose family I lured here."

"Me?" Emily asked. "You thought I would kill Sophie?"

"Of course, you idiot," he said. "You almost did the other night, when the two of you nearly tore each other apart after you ate that poor Senator's son."

All three went slack-jawed. "You were there?" Emily asked.

"I tend to stop into my unoccupied properties to make sure local teens weren't using them for parties or drug dens," he said. "I was just shutting off the lights when I saw Tate creeping around into the backyard through the window. I must say, it was impressive to watch both of you in your true forms."

"But we didn't kill each other," said Emily.

"You would have, if the witch hadn't appeared," said Griess. "But there's always now. Emily, you are the perfect weapon. An angry, hormonal, teenage she-wolf with an uncontrollable desire to kill and feed. Marry that with centuries of hatred and abuse between your kinds, and, bloodshed is inevitable."

"Just like between the Egyptians and Hebrews?" Morgan said sharply. "Didn't work to well for your people the last time, according to some texts."

"You didn't lure me here," said Emily, scrunching up her face. "My dad's work brought us here."

"Ah, that's right," Griess said. "A professor at an obscure community college in the middle of New Mexico gets offered the perfect job in South Carolina without even an interview. And it's near the island where they just happen to have an empty house waiting. Yes, completely random chance."

"How could you even know I existed?" Emily asked, not wanting to believe what he was implying, that he'd somehow used her family as pawns in some weird, sick game.

"Now that part truly was coincidence," he said. "I was in New Mexico to see a traveling Egyptian exhibit at a museum in Albuquerque. I'm always on the lookout for my step-brother, you know. If I ever find his sarcophagus, I'm going to resurrect him just to kill him myself."

"How about looking for a good therapist instead?" said Sophie.

"Sophie, stop," Morgan hissed.

"The local news was all a flutter over a strange animal attack in a small town called Portales," Griess continued, ignoring her. "The local authorities had never seen such savagery. I knew at once what must've done it. I drove to Portales immediately and found the lone survivor in Intensive Care. Never leave survivors, silly girl."

He waived a finger at her in mocking fashion.

"I woke him up long enough to extract what had happened. It just so happens before he blacked out that night, he saw the monster that attacked them fall to the ground and shrivel up into a beautiful, raven-haired young woman. He also described a mysterious man in a minivan who had shot him in the face with a high-powered pellet gun."

Emily couldn't disguise the fear in her face at the idea of her dad being exposed in all this.

"I assume that was dear old dad," Griess said. "Don't worry. The young man didn't live long enough to share that encounter with anyone else. But I stayed around Portales. I waited. I heard locals tell of other attacks. No survivors in those, of course. That poor school teacher, and *her dog*. So cruel. Such unbridled violence. You felt no kinship with the creature whatsoever, Emily?"

"Shut up," Emily growled at him, fighting back tears of guilt that were trying to squeeze their way out. She could feel her emotions getting the better of her. This man would never get near her father, she thought, whatever she had to do to guarantee it.

"Then late one night, I saw a middle-aged white man driving a minivan through a neighborhood in which he clearly didn't belong. I followed him as he stopped at a park and scooped up the body of a young beauty, and cradled her as only a father might, placing her lovingly in the back of his vehicle." His eyes narrowed as he stared at Emily. It sent a creeped out shiver up her spine.

"From there, the rest was simple. I found out who he was, and who you were. Upon my return to South Carolina, I paid a visit to the directors of the University laboratory. They were soon convinced they needed Adam Morrison on staff immediately."

"You son of a bitch," Emily seethed through clenched teeth. She felt Morgan wrap a hand around her arm, but she didn't care. She was trembling with anger. "Don't you dare even say my dad's name again."

"Finish the work I brought you here for, and I promise, your daddy will be fine," Griess smiled. "Perhaps the witch will help you. She's got a mother to protect too."

"Fuck you," Morgan's eyes blazed.

"Just kill her, here and now," he said, pointing at Sophie. "The witch can subdue her long enough for you to tear her to pieces. Then with every drop of her immortal blood, I will grow stronger and more powerful."

"Will that actually work?" Morgan asked Sophie.

"He seems to think so," she answered. "It certainly keeps Luther feeling spry. Are you really going to kill me to find out?"

"Of course not," said Morgan. She winked at Sophie. "Screw this *fuckboy*. We can take him."

"I'm not touching Sophie and neither is Morgan," Emily said to Griess. "You leave Lune de Sang. Leave South Carolina. Leave the country. And the three of us won't shred you right here in your own kitchen. Go find another werewolf and another vampire if you want, but you are not allowed back here."

"Wretched girls don't get to give orders to a man like me," he retorted. "I am here to stay. This island is where I will erect my palace and sit on my golden throne. And all your people will bow before me."

He reached into the box he had set on the counter. He lifted out a wide blue and gold striped head dress and put it on over his hair. The sides fanned out around him like the flaps of a cobra. Fitting, as a gold serpent rose from the front above his brow.

Then Griess removed a long metal case which he unlatched and removed a jeweled gold collar which he fastened around his neck and let rest across his chest.

"Going to a Halloween party?" Sophie smirked.

"This, you insolent devil's whore, is the authentic attire of my royal ancestry," he said with a regal flourish. "It is the garb of one chosen to be a god."

"Does anyone else feel like they've gone completely insane?" Sophie asked with a laugh, looking around at the other two.

"Filthy demon," Griess hissed at her, pulling the dagger from his belt. "After they kill you, I will cut out your tongue and cook it."

"Ooh, you're kinky," Sophie said, flicking it out at him.

"You do look like one of the robots in the *Curse of the Pharaohs* ride at Dinsmore's Adventure Kingdoms," Emily added in disbelief.

"I've had enough," screamed Griess. He lifted the golden ankh above his head. "*Damned servants awaken and come forth now at my command.*"

The girls waited for something, though they had no clue what it might be. All was quiet. They looked at each other and Sophie shrugged.

"This is stupid," Sophie said. "He can't really summon an army of the dead. Let's take him."

No sooner had she finished her sentence when windows all over the house began to shatter. There was something pounding violently on the back door of the house.

"What the hell's happening?" Emily asked her friends.

But they both looked just as confused, and alarmed, eyes darting all over. Soon they saw who, or what was causing he commotion.

Rotten corpses and skeletal bodies of men and women with dark gray, leathery flesh wearing the threadbare ragged remains of their Sunday finery began climbing through the broken windows and splintering the doors to get inside.

They were a mob of hanging eyeballs and exposed, yellowed teeth. If not for their ragged suits and dresses, it would be hard to tell the males from the females. But in this condition, they were equally terrifying.

"Zombies now?" Sophie yelled. "Are you fucking kidding me?"

The room filled with a horrid, dank smell of decay. The reanimated dead staggered with boney hands swinging and grabbing for the girls, like marionettes with unseen strings.

Zombies seemed to be pouring into the house from every

direction. There were over a dozen putrid smelling zombies inside the house, slowly advancing on the girls, making undecipherable moaning sounds as they bumped into each other.

"I realize they don't look like much of an army now," said Griess. "They have lain forgotten, deep within the soil for a century. When my new kingdom is restored, I've promised them that their earthly bodies will be as well. When my palace rises on the spot where the Levasseur manor now sits, they will each have a role of great esteem at my court, in exchange for removing any obstacles in my way."

"Obstacles?" Morgan asked. "You mean us?"

"We need a plan here ladies," said Sophie, ruby eyes blazing and fangs exposed. Her fingers were splayed with unsheathed claws at the tips.

"Morgan," said Emily. "Do you think that wind spell you used on those cops will work on these things?"

"I can try it," said Morgan, wiggling her fingers as if preparing to go to work.

"You're wasting time," said Griess. "These unfortunate souls are not the ones you need to worry about. The vampire is the threat. Do you really think she looks at you as a friend, or as *food*? When your back is turned, she will sink her fangs into your neck and drain you too."

"Don't listen to him Morgan," said Emily "He's trying to divide us."

"No," said Morgan, looking from Sophie to the zombies, and back at Griess. "No she won't."

"She will murder you, and your mother," said Griess. "She can't control the evil inside her. I can."

"And even if you're right, I'm willing to take the chance," said Morgan. "She is my friend. I have to trust her."

"Trust," he spat. "I trusted my brother. Look what happened. Now use your spell to subdue her so the wolf can dismember her. Then I will call off these zombies. You'd better hurry. The poor Morrison family doesn't have much time."

"Huh?" Emily jerked her head back and glared at him. "What did you say?"

"Emily ignore him," said Sophie. "He's trying to trigger you so you'll wolf out."

"Am I?" Griess taunted. "Step out into my back yard. The custom fire pit is enormous. Great for those occasional cool winter nights. It's quite a selling point. But oh, a small child, such as poor little Grant, could so easily fall in."

With a nauseous feeling twisting in her stomach, Emily ran for the backdoor, knocking uncoordinated ghouls out of her way as she did. She threw open the back door. Her scream at what she saw echoed into the night.

Adam Morrison, her mom Lorrie, and her little brother Grant were kneeling in the wet grass in the middle of the yard. Their hands and ankles were bound behind their backs. Each was being held down by two or three zombies that grunted and growled as they tried to struggle free.

In the center of the yard was a concrete patio with a deep stone fire pit. Orange flames danced and snapped inside, casting an orange glow across her family members' frightened faces. She could see sweet little Grant, who always looked happy – or at least mischievous – was terrified. Tears were streaming down his cheeks.

Her dad's head snapped up when her heard her. She could see blood running down his face.

"Emily, get out of here," he cried out. "It's not safe for you . . . *ungh*." A rotted fist knocked him across the forehead. The zombie then pushed his face into the grass.

"Do as I command, " Griess ordered from behind her. "Your parents needn't lose either of their children tonight. Continue to refuse my command, and their child, their *real* child, will perishes in fire. A fate that I can only imagine is the most painful way to die possible."

Emily began to weep. This was her fault. She'd allowed her family to be put in danger, because of what she was. It would have been better if Sophie *had* killed her that night near the pool.

"Emily," Sophie called to her. She and Morgan were also seeing what had been done to her family through the broken windows of the living room.

"It's fine. Just do it."

Chapter 16

Emily turned to see her beautiful vampire friend standing in the backdoor of the house. For the first time since they'd met, Sophie actually looked solemn; even sad. Her eyes glistened as if she too were about to cry. Something Emily didn't know vampires were capable of.

"Transform," Sophie said. She raised her hands out at her sides. "Change into the wolf and kill me. I won't fight. You need your family."

Emily looked at her friend with panic. She could no more kill Sophie now than she could her own mother. She wanted to say so, but she couldn't find the words. She just shook her head frantically, tears flowing from her eyes.

"It's okay," Sophie said. "Honestly, I've had two centuries of this life. I'm good. This planet isn't going to get any better. Not for someone like me. Just do it, and free them."

"Free them for what?" Emily cried out. "A world where this psychopath is a god? No. I can't. I won't."

"Sophie's right Emily," said Morgan, standing behind her. "You need to change. Right now. It's time for the wolf. It's the only way."

"I mean, I thought you might argue a little," Sophie couldn't help but mumble with a forced smile.

Morgan was staring at Emily's frightened eyes. This time, she spoke directly to her mind without opening her mouth.

"Trust me. Just change."

"How?" Emily asked. "I don't think I can do it at will."

"Think of what they'll do to Grant if you don't."

It was the worst thing she'd ever heard. The idea of picturing these horrible abominations dragging her precious eight-year-old brother to the edge of the pit and throwing his little body into the flames. It was too deep. He'd never be able to pull himself out. Tears flooded her eyes.

And then, it happened. Her body began to tremble. Her muscles swelled. The bones and ligaments stretched and twisted. The hair began to sprout. As Emily had warned, the steely muscles of her thighs tore the stitching out of the red leather pants.

Griess saw the transformation happening and began to laugh outload.

"Yes," he cried out. He raised his dagger in triumph. "It begins."

With this monster, he would fulfil his divine right to rule.

While the wolf killed the vampire, he would cut the witch's throat, and as soon as the wolf became human again, he would remove her head.

After all, he had learned one lesson from his perfidious half-brother. He needed to remove all threats to his rule immediately.

And his servants would have to kill the family as well. They were inconsequential without the wolf girl, but why let them live? And he would need an offering for the gods.

"Grant, close your eyes closed," Adam Morrison called out to his son. "Don't look at your sister, buddy. Everything's going to be okay. Just . . . shut your eyes."

It was too late. The child had stopped crying. Now he staring in disbelief at the strange sight of his sister turning into some kind of monster his parents had heretofore assured him didn't exist.

"Grant, listen to daddy," Lorie added, swallowing hard.

She stared past her daughter at the man in Egyptian attire. The one who's hand she'd shaken not so long ago. The one who took such a keen interest in their family as they ate lunch. The one who'd somehow managed to slip by her usually keen instinct for danger.

She made a mental note. That would never happen again.

"Everything will be okay," Lorie assured her little boy. She glared at Griess feeling a fireball of hatred welling up in her stomach. "I promise you, son. No one is going to hurt you today, or Emmy."

Just as Emily's muzzle filled with sharp, animal teeth and the flesh-tearing claws extended from her fingers, Morgan knew she had to take action. She ran into the living room and climbed up into a window sill, scraping her arms on jagged shards of broken glass stuck in the frame. She winced as it pierced her flesh, but knew she had to push the pain aside.

Sophie could smell the fresh blood running down Morgan's arms and turned back into the house to see the witch leaning out of the window, extending her arms. Sophie took note of the multiple zombies shuffling around the house, closing in on them.

"Um, Morgan," she said. "If you've got a plan, the time is now."

Morgan held one hand out flat, and the other straight up above, pressing her wrists together and making a V-shape.

"Please let this work," she whispered.

Morgan had thought of an incantation she'd read about, but had always been reticent to use it, because of its origins. It was older than the Celtic witches. Older than Druids.

It had almost been lost to the sands of time, until it was rediscovered in more recent years, during a darker time, by a bad man who possessed no real powers of his own, but hoped to harness it nonetheless, and use it as a weapon. He assembled a team to translate it to his native tongue.

But merely speaking the words wasn't enough to make them

work, praise the Goddess. Words had no power on their own. Only a witch of extraordinary power and purpose would be able to wield this spell.

Hoping she was worthy of this magick, Morgan recited the German translation: *"Ein rechtschaffenes Feuer der Götter bewohnt meine Hände. Gib mir die Kraft, die Welt vom Unreinen zu befreien!"*

Her eyes turned orange as fire erupted from between her palms, shooting forward into the night. The flames passed right over Emily's family and engulfed the zombies' heads and torsos. The reanimated goons began to flail their arms and stumble around, shrieking in pain. One fell right over the stone ledge into the burning pit.

The zombies that had threatened Emily's family were quickly scattered, or burnt to a crisp.

"Emily," Morgan whispered, eyes shut, confident her friend's keen wolf ears would hear her. "They're safe now. Griess is all yours."

Morgan slipped back down out of the window. Her still blazing eyes took stock of the rotting undead townsfolk shuffling toward them to attack. "Sophie, these guys are ours."

"What? You want me to bite these things?" Sophie said. "That's gross."

"You don't have to bite," Morgan rolled her eyes. "You're super strong, remember? Tear their heads off."

"Oh, right," said Sophie, nodding. "That I can do."

Sophie leapt forward at two of them and bashed their heads together, shattering their fragile skulls. She then set about ripping their arms off.

Morgan turned to another batch of ghouls and raised her hands, blasting them with javelins of fire. They bellowed painful moans as they burned, and fell all over themselves, rolling around the floor in a blazing mass. Within seconds the thick carpet began to burn too.

"*Shit*," Morgan said, "I didn't think about that!"

"Ugh, Morgan what did you do?" Sophie called out from across the room as she was breaking zombie legs off. She looked back at her friend. "It smells like burnt dog hair in . . . *oh, I see*. Interesting choice."

Outside the house, Emily understood that her family was no longer in immediate danger. The black she-wolf slowly turned and growled at the man in the funny striped headdress.

Griess suddenly understood he was no longer in the position of power he'd hoped for. He began to shuffle backward, nervously waiving his dagger at her.

"Stay away," he hissed. Griess could see the orange glow of fire rising inside the house. His forces were diminished and his house appeared to be burning to the ground. That didn't matter, he told himself.

He was going to build a colossal palace out of the mortals' own gold that would cover two-thirds of the island. And he still had the Dagger of Ra.

"Don't forget Emily," Griess spat, "I can summon an army of the undead. This ankh can open a portal to the underworld and summon forth a demon horde. Your family isn't safe. You've only delayed the inevitable. Kill the vampire, now, or you all die."

The werewolf stood, ready to lunge. Her chest heaved.

And then a gunshot rang out in the night. Griess fell over, grabbing for his arm and dropping the dagger. Luther had appeared from around the side of the house, running as fast as a man Luther's size could move, and having quickly assessed the situation, buried a bullet in Griess' forearm.

Luther wrapped one thick hand around the guy in the headdress and loincloth's neck and slammed his meaty, ring-lined fist into his face. Griess folded to the ground, a mess of bloody goo where his nose had been.

"Sophie, where're you at?" Luther called out, keeping his eyes behind his black lenses trained on the dark killing machine watching him carefully with a constant low pitched growl. He wasn't sure if she remembered him, and whether it would be a good thing or a bad thing if she did.

"Luther, you came," Sophie grinned, appearing in the doorway of the house, backlit by fire, and seeing her mountainous manservant outside, brandishing his pistol.

Luther charged toward the burning house like a rhino, and grabbed her around the waist, hoisting her into the air. "It's time to go home. No more sleepovers for you."

Then Luther saw Morgan still inside, using a wind spell to keep the flames that were now climbing the walls and spreading across the carpet from burning her alive. She had backed herself into a corner, literally.

"Yo," Luther called out, "witch girl. The truck is running."

Morgan was relieved to see the hulking brute. She spread her hands out in the air, chanting, and creating a path through the fire to the backdoor.

She ran toward Luther and Sophie, as with every step she took forward, the flames closed back in behind her. She stopped casting and leapt into the air, feeling his hefty arm wrap around her and toss her over his other shoulder.

Luther dropped both of them, a little less than carefully, on the grass outside. He gestured his head toward Emily, looming over Griess, snarling.

"Can you turn full moon fever over there back into a person. I'm not letting her in the truck like that. She'll tear up the leather seats."

"Sophie, can you take care of Emily's family?" Morgan asked. "I'll work on bringing Emily back down."

"What do we do with *Imhotep*?" asked Sophie, rolling her eyes toward Griess, who was still out cold in the grass.

Morgan thought for a second. The right thing to do would probably be get everyone to safety, including Griess.

"To hell with him," she said instead.

"I like you more every minute," Sophie smiled. She leapt through the air, crossing the yard, and landing beside Emily's family.

"Emily," Morgan said softly, walking toward her friend with her palms exposed. "It's okay now. We don't need the wolf anymore. You can let it rest."

Emily stared through glassy green eyes. She made no movement as Morgan approached and slowly raised a hand to place it on her head.

"It's me babe," she said. "You don't want to hurt me. We're friends. Your family is okay. We can all go home."

The wolf closed her eyes and her body began to relax.

Morgan felt a tinge of elation. Emily actually heard, and was somehow able to control the beast within.

Slowly, Emily dropped to her knees. Her thick, taught flesh loosened. Her skeleton returned to its natural state. The hair receded. Her face was again restored to that of an attractive human countenance. In a moment, Emily, naked, shivering, but human once more, collapsed unconscious into Morgan's arms.

"That is so freaky," said Luther. "Come on, I'll help you get her into the truck. We have to get out of here."

Morgan nodded and closed her eyes for a brief embrace with her friend. She stroked Emily's hair. She couldn't imagine the emotions this girl had gone through in just the last few hours alone.

Selfishly Morgan couldn't help but hope that at least one of those emotions might have been for her. But she shook the idea out of her head. She shouldn't think about that. This was not the appropriate moment.

Then she heard a cry that sounded like a wounded bear.

Luther dropped to his knees. Griess was standing over him, his head dress off and his greasy hair hanging in his face. Blood was still spilling from his smashed nose.

He had plunged the curved dagger into Luther's leg and sliced it around, severing ligaments behind his knee. The big man was instantly immobilized.

Even wounded, Luther tried to swing his arm around and fire at his attacker. Griess had pulled a stone paver from the fire pit and smashed it against Luther's head, knocking him flat on the ground.

"You have been a problem for me every step of the way," Griess spat at Morgan. "Know that the blood of your dear friend's family will be on your hands. If you hadn't inserted yourself in the wolf girl's life in the hope of fulfilling your own Sapphic fantasy, they wouldn't have to die today. And neither would you. Now you'll be lucky if I only *kill* your dear mother. But the rest of you are already dead. Even the boy."

"We will never kill Sophie," Morgan shouted. "You're powerless against us Griess."

"Not while I have this," he said, brandishing the ankh. "The dagger gives me all the power I need. I have armies beneath the earth just waiting for my command."

"But you're still not immortal, Mr. Griess," said a woman's voice behind him.

A hand grabbed his wrist and, twisting it behind his back, yanked his shoulder out of its socket. Griess screamed at the searing pain of something ripping into the flesh of his forearm, exploding veins, and forcing him to release the ankh. It landed on the patio with a metallic clang.

After a moment, his arm was released and Griess stumbled forward, unable to straighten his arm properly.

The woman who had attacked him whipped her head back in a flourish of brown hair. Her eyes filled with blood, glowing red like cornelian stones under her furrowed brow.

There was no mistaking they were the eyes of a vampire, just like Sophie's, and yet perhaps, even brighter. They hadn't shone like that in a long time. It had been years since she'd let her own inner-demon loose.

It was Lorie Morrison, Emily's mother. Blood ran down her chin, staining her faded Eastern New Mexico University sweatshirt.

Griess stared in disbelief. Lorie spit his blood back into his face and wiped her mouth with her hand. "I wouldn't drink your expired blood if I were actually dying."

Morgan was speechless. She actually wondered if she had been knocked out, or was still in the house, succumbing to smoke inhalation, and this was some kind of hallucination.

"Morgan," Sophie called, running up from the side of the house. "Emily's dad and brother are fine, but her crazy mom took . . . *off.*"

Sophie froze as well when she saw Lorie standing there, tight grip on Amman's arm, with viper-like fangs dripping crimson from her mouth.

"Sophie," Morgan screamed in a whisper. "Did you do this?"

"Hell no," Sophie gasped. "I had nothing to do with it. I've never even met her. And I don't turn people. Especially not the parents of my friends."

"Relax ladies," said Lorie. "I've been hiding my own secret since long before either of you was born. Even you, Sophie. I thought when I left Lune de Sang, I could bury if forever. But this damn place has some kind of power, doesn't it?"

"This is crazy," Sophie said in disbelief. "I'm assuming Emily doesn't know. What . . . what about your husband?"

"No way," Lorie answered. "I debated telling him, but I was afraid it would scare him off. Then fate decided it would be funny to give us a werewolf daughter. I can't tell him now. Speaking of, where are my boys?"

"They're coming," said Sophie. "Your son was pretty shaken up. Is he, you know, one of us?"

"I'm not sure yet," Lorie sighed. "I hope not. He hasn't shown any signs. But neither of them needs to know about this. Or Emily." Her face turned very stern – almost menacing. "Do you both understand me?"

Both girls nodded.

"How did this happen to you?" Morgan asked. "When?"

"That's a complicated question," Lorie chuckled. She looked directly at Sophie. "You may not know this, but your father, Monsieur Levasseur, had many lovers."

"That's no secret," Sophie said.

"And he had other kids," said Lorie. "After you, and before."

Morgan gasped as it sank in. "Levasseur was your father too?"

Lorie nodded.

"What?" Sophie took a breath. "Hold up. You're . . . ."

"The daughter," said Morgan suddenly. "All the stories about Levasseur say he came to the island with a young girl. His daughter."

"It's true," said Lorie. "I'm the mysterious daughter. We're sisters, Sophie."

"I can't . . . this is insane," Sophie said, trying to make sense of this new information. "I have a sister?"

"Relax," Lorie laughed. "You look like you've seen a ghost, which, around here might be true. I realize it's a lot, and, probably not the best timing. Let's talk about it later. Right now we need to do something with this one."

She kicked Griess in the side. "I need to collect my family," Lorie continued, "and they cannot see me like this. Griess is all yours."

Lorie dragged him by the wrist and slid him across the concrete to Sophie's feet.

Two vampires on the island was something Griess had never expected. He pressed a hand to the bleeding puncture wounds on his neck.

And the wolf girl was no longer useful. Defeated, at least for now, he resigned himself to the knowledge there was nothing else to do but to plead for his life.

"Please, don't do this," he begged Sophie. "We can share the new kingdom together. Imagine being a vampire queen. Kill her, and her animal daughter. She is a threat to you. To your power. I can help you rule."

Sophie bent down and looked at him with a smile. She pursed her lips as if considering his offer, then shook her head.

Without a word, she dropped her jaw and sunk her fangs into the other side of his neck, tearing through his jugular. He squealed like an injured piglet and tried to squirm loose.

Sophie bit down even harder and yanked her head back, much the way she'd watched Emily do, and removed a three inch chuck of flesh and vein from his neck and spat it into the air.

Blood sprayed everywhere. Morgan ducked for cover with Emily clutched to her chest.

Griess' coloring began to change from tan and smooth to gray and leathery. His flesh and muscle began to shrivel and rot away as his blood evaporated.

The wound in his neck turned from ruby red to black and slimy. He tried to let off one last scream as he painfully morphed from a healthy man to a 3,000 year old corpse.

The ground around Griess transformed into sand. Yellow smoke escaped from the earth as the smell of sulfur filled the air. Screams of torture could be heard crying out from somewhere far below. Shadowy clawed hands burst from the ground and gripped his limbs, tearing at his body.

Two more hands grabbed at his golden collar and broke the chain that fastened it, throwing it aside. As another hand snatched him by the hair, a hideous serpent like something from a nightmare materialized and began to slither around his neck, over and under, constricting around his body and drawing his limbs taught, and squeezed. Griess' eyes popped from his skull and rolled across the patio.

When Griess was completely engulfed by the serpent, it melted into a black linen, leaving the former prince-turned - realtor completely wrapped from head to toe. The demonic hands gripped the newly mummified man and dragged him down through the sand into the underworld.

If Prince Thutmose had cheated death once, Amman Griess would not. This time, it seemed, the underworld intended to keep him. The sand devoured him, and the earth became dirt and grass once again.

While everyone else stared at the place where Griess had just been pulled into the netherworld, Lorie Morrison picked up the ankh. With the curved blade, she cut a small line across her finger then threw the artifact aside. She bent down beside

Luther and squeezed her blood into the deep wound on his leg that had been rapidly draining him of his life giving liquid.

Within seconds the tendons reformed and the skin closed back up. Slowly, she helped him to his feet with one hand as if he weighed no more than a toddler. Luther nodded his appreciation.

"Thank you for caring about my daughter," Lorie said, crossing to Morgan and kneeling beside her. Her eyes met with those of the curly haired witch.

"You're a very special girl, Morgan Bassett," she said. "I sensed it the first time I saw you at the school. I bet you would've sniffed me out, if Emily's pheromones weren't so wild and strong. And since then, well, I think your mind has been elsewhere." Lorie smiled softly and stroked Emily's hair.

"I wish I could tell her the truth about myself," she continued. "Can you even calculate the odds? A barren vampire unknowingly adopts a werewolf. For now, she has you now, to help her. I am happy for that."

Inside the house, the ceiling collapsed as the flames had engulfed the walls.

"We need to go," Luther called out. "This thing's starting to rage. Somebody's going to dial 9-1-1 any minute."

"The big guy's right," said Lorie, helping Morgan support Emily. "This place is going down. Time for me to go back to playing mommy and housewife."

They all made their way around the house as Grant came running toward them with Adam close behind.

"Mommy," Grant called. He jumped up into her arms just as her fangs slid back into her soft gums. She held him tight and comforted her boy.

"I told you we'd be okay," she whispered to her son. "Emily's good too. She just hit her head. She's going to be fine. We all are."

"Why is she naked?" Grant asked.

"Umm, well, that's a good question," Lorie thought. "She used her clothes to tie up those zombies. But they're all dead now. Isn't your sister brave?"

The three girls and Luther trailed her. All helping to carry Emily.

"Yeah, she's awesome," said Grant, happily buying the fib.

Adam Morrison hugged his family tightly then went to Emily's side. She was starting to stir. "I can take her from here."

"I'd like to help," said Morgan. "I mean, if it's okay."

Adam looked at her and then felt his wife's gaze on his back. He turned to look at her and she gave him a nod and mouthed that it was.

"Uh, sure, thanks," he said. "Thank you for being such a good friend to her, Morgan."

Luther helped them load Emily into his truck cab with her

head on Morgan's lap and her legs across her parents'. Grant would have been thrilled to ride in the bed of the truck but his parents made him sit inside, on the floor, where he was out of sight.

Sophie sat up front, still processing the strange twist the night had taken.

Luther tore out of the driveway with the lights off and drove down the dark street as the orange glow of the fire began to reflect in the windows. The entire mansion was now engulfed in flames. No one said a word during the short drive to the other side of the island.

Sophie kept staring into the rear view mirror for a glimpse of Emily's mom – her sister. She was overwhelmed at the idea of having a sibling. Although she could hardly comprehend the fact that it made Emily her niece.

Sophie was never all that comfortable with the concept of family. She hadn't really had one for most of her existence.

The truck stopped in front of the Morrison's house. They heard sirens from firetrucks barreling over the bridge.

Dr. Morrison and Morgan helped the groggy Emily out of the car. Lorie crossed over to the passenger side, behind Sophie.

"Is she going to be alright?" Sophie asked. She wasn't sure what else she was supposed to say. This was one of those moments where, despite her 200 years of existence, she felt like a confused, frightened teenager.

"She'll be fine," said Lorie. She touched her hand against

Sophie's cheek. "So will you. We will talk soon, I promise. Maybe I can fill in some of your gaps."

"Okay," Sophie nodded, with tears in her eyes. "But don't you think Emily should know?"

"Eventually," Lorie nodded. "But we need to get her situation figured out first. All this would probably be too much for her right now."

"It's almost too much for me," Sophie nodded, giving her a faint smile.

Lorie nodded and smiled back. She patted her hand. "Fair enough."

Morgan walked back down to the truck once Emily's dad had taken Emily inside. She was dabbing at her eyes with her sleeve. It had been an overwhelming night for all of them.

"You want a ride home?" Sophie offered. "Better yet, you could just come crash at my place. I've got like three or four guest rooms."

"Really?" Morgan asked, sounding unsure. "Yeah, that would be good."

"No," said Lorie. Both girls looked over to see her walking back to the truck. "Morgan, I'd like it if you stayed here tonight with our family. It would be good if you were here when she wakes up."

"I'd like that," Morgan said, surprised. "Sophie, uh, I'm going to . . . you know."

"Go," Sophie said. She smiled and waved her off.

"We'll come by tomorrow."

"If you must," Sophie sighed, and then immediately laughed. "Just remember, I sleep late."

Lorie put her arm around Morgan's shoulders and they walked together toward the house in silence.

"You good?" Luther asked staring straight ahead through his black glasses as he shifted the truck back into drive.

"Of course," Sophie answered staring out the window.

She could see the firelight over the rooftops and trees. The sirens were growing louder. By morning there'd be little left of the house. Only charred beams and ash. And stacks of stolen gold covered in ash.

"Maybe you're right," Sophie said, staring absently out the windshield. "Maybe we should leave the island for a while. This place will be crawling with cops as soon as the firemen find that gold."

"Plus the FBI," said Luther. "And the media won't be far behind."

"Those too," she said.

Leaving would probably be smart. But the truth was, for once, Sophie hated the thought of leaving Lune de Sang. She had friends here now. In fact, she had a family.

"That reminds me," said Luther. He dug underneath his seat. After a second, he lifted up the ankh dagger. "It didn't feel right leaving this behind."

"Luther, I'm surprised at you," she smiled. "That should probably be in a museum or something."

"Do you want to take it to a museum?" he asked.

"Hell no," Sophie laughed. "Might be useful one day. You never know when you might need to summon an army of the undead."

"I'll lock it up in the vault when we get home," Luther said.

They drove around the corner, away from the direction all the fire trucks, police cars, and ambulances were headed, and into the alley that ran behind Sophie's block.

They made it back to the house without any trouble, and Luther took the ankh to a secret room under the house. Outside of the heavy lead door was a monitor with an eye rest similar to that of a microscope. He took off his sunglasses and pressed his face against it.

After a quick green light slide across his eyes, a panel opened. There was a digital key pad. This vault was even more secure than the *pantry* upstairs. It had to be.

He punched in the code. 0-5-2-6-1-8-9-7-#.

Inside, Luther found a spot on a shelf beside some other jeweled antiquities. He gave the room a quick look. There were original paintings by artists like Monet and Gauguin. There was a sword with the name Vlad III etched into the handle. There were stacks of banded money, of multiple denominations, and various currencies.

And a number of boxes and cases, the contents of which even Luther did not know. He actually preferred it that way.

Luther flipped off the light and stepped out of the vault. The heavy door slid shut with a thud behind him.

Epilogue

Ella Bassett woke the next morning and poked her head into her daughter's room. For a split second she thought perhaps Morgan had come home last night after all, given the state of the unmade bed.

Then quickly it dawned on her that this fact was significant of nothing. Her daughter never made her bed. Normally Ella wouldn't worry, but this morning she couldn't help but feel some uneasiness lingering in the air.

Ella scooped some small crystals off of the desk. She sat on the edge of Morgan's bed, closed her eyes, juggling the clear stones in her hand and hugging one of her daughter's pillows.

After a moment she was confident Morgan was just fine. Ella wasn't sure what had happened, but a wave of comfort washed over her, as if to assure her that if Morgan and her new friends had indeed run into trouble in the night, they had managed to overcome it.

But there was something more than that. The strange feeling

Ella had been experiencing for a long time now was suddenly gone. No, not gone. Just, different. The air smelled sweeter. The sliver of sunlight penetrating her daughter's curtains seemed brighter. She felt warmth emanating from the crystal in her hand.

Whatever unwelcome presence she was certain had settled in Lune de Sang seemed to have moved on. Or been removed. Some new power was present. New, but also familiar. It had returned.

Feeling optimistic, Ella Bassett dressed, made herself a cup of English Breakfast with a dash of hemp oil, and headed downstairs to prepare the shop for opening.

Rather than turn on the lights, Ella opted to open the shades over the big storefront window to flood the store with sunshine. She much preferred natural light and the playful shadows it cast than artificial fluorescents.

As she pulled the chord and the heavy shade lifted, she was startled by a man standing just outside on the sidewalk. The stranger's back was to the store, only inches from the glass.

He wore a black cowboy hat with feathers in the band. A long braid of thick black and gray hair ran down the back of his worn denim jacket.

As if he'd heard Ella's startled squeal, he wheeled around. He was an older Native American man, with a rugged, tan face weathered by a lifetime of adventures. He gave her a timid smile and his kind, dark eyes seemed to sparkle. Ella found him quite handsome.

The man wore a wide pewter belt buckle inlaid with turquoise stones. He also wore a silver chain with an eagle pendant resting against his chest. He gave her a quick wave.

Ella waved back and gestured toward the door as if to ask if he wanted to come inside. He nodded. Ella crossed the floor, unlocked the shop door, and opened it.

"Good morning," the man said in a husky voice. "I'm sorry if I startled you."

"Oh it's quite alright," Ella smiled. "Please. Come in."

"Much obliged," he nodded, tipping his hat and walking past her to enter the store. "I suppose I'm not what your typical customer looks like."

As he crossed the threshold, Ella felt a rush of energy. Not good or bad, but powerful and intoxicating.

"All good spirits are welcome in my store," she said. "Is there something specific you're looking for? A gift perhaps?"

"Well, no," he answered, looking around the shop. "Not something. More like someone. My name is Russell Night Eagle. I believe my granddaughter may have been spending some time around here lately."

"Your granddaughter?" Ella repeated. "Emily?"

Ella immediately cursed her own tongue. She hadn't meant to just blurt out Emily's name. She didn't know this man, or his intentions, even if he did cast a kind aura. But it did suddenly seem so obvious. He was Native American, and his clothing indicated he had come from somewhere out west.

"You do know her then?" he said, his eyes widening. "Please, is she here? I've been so worried."

"No, I'm sorry," said Ella. "She and my daughter stayed with a friend last night. Was she expecting a visit?"

"No, I doubt that," Russell chuckled. "Emily doesn't know me. I've never even seen her. My daughter gave her up for adoption as soon as she was born, for fear of what she might become. What, I fear, she may have already become."

"I'm not sure what you mean," Ella tried to bluff.

Clearly, he knew the truth about Emily. But that didn't mean she shouldn't be careful to protect her daughter's friend until she knew more about him. As he had just admitted, he had never even known his granddaughter. Why was he suddenly looking for her?

"Why don't you tell me how Emily can reach you and I'll have my daughter pass it along to her when she gets back."

"Please, ma'am," he said, "I swear to you I don't mean her any harm. Just the opposite. I'm not here to cause any trouble or break up the family she knows. I am indebted to them. I only want to see her. I'm sure she's got questions. Emily is going through something very difficult, and uncommon. She needs guidance. The kind, in this case, only a blood relative can give her."

The older man had tears forming in his endless obsidian eyes. Ella couldn't help but listen to her intuition. She invited Russell upstairs to the apartment for some tea and zucchini bread. They talked for what turned into hours.

Russell Night Eagle explained how he'd manage to track down where Emily's adoptive family lived by watching the news. He had learned her adoptive father was a doctor, but assumed that meant the medical kind.

He was about to leave Portales when, on a whim, he asked a talkative waitress if she knew of any local doctors that had adopted Indian daughters.

He said the spirits were guiding him that day, because the girl had immediately said: "No, but that's so weird. I used to babysit for this professor whose daughter was part Native American. They just moved to South Carolina or something."

Russell said he did some more digging and discovered a Dr. Adam Morrison had just left his position at the local college. He called the school's science department claiming to have a package for Morrison with no forwarding address.

It took a couple attempts, but finally some harried lab assistant let it slip that Morrison had taken a "sweet research gig" at school in Charleston.

"I am impressed by your research skills," Ella told him. "And your tenacity."

"Well, my people were great trackers," Russell grinned and bowed his head. "I just had to find her."

The two of them continued chatting like old friends. They had so little in common but found each other fascinating. Ella had so much admiration and respect for Native America culture and mysticism.

And Russell told her bluntly he'd never met a witch before. But he had known many Shaman.

"May I ask something personal?" Ella asked him.

"Am I what Emily is?" he said, knowing what her question would be.

"I'm sorry," she said, feeling she'd pried too far.

"No, it's fine," Russell told her. "I am. But it's been a long time since I've succumbed to it. As I got older, it became easier to contain."

"Have all your ancestors been this way?" she asked.

"No," he said quickly, now seeming upset. "This thing is not natural. We have our legends and myths, but this, it is not the same. This was done to us. My whole village."

"Dear goddess," Ella whispered. "Done by who?"

"Uncle Sam," he answered after a moment, as if not sure what to tell her. "I was little. The army came to our reservation in the night. Rounded up many. My whole family. Men, women, children; it didn't matter."

"That's awful," she said, fighting emotion. "Why?"

"The country was at war," Russell Night Eagle explained. "Hitler was trying to create monsters. I guess the President decided to do the same. Couldn't experiment on whites, but us Indians were considered expendable."

"I am so sorry," said Ella.

"You didn't do anything," Russell said. "You weren't even alive yet. And I have given away my anger. I am old and don't want to carry it. But I must help my granddaughter while I can."

"I will help you," Ella said, taking his rough hand. "Whatever I can do."

They'd completely lost track of time, having finished their tea, and half a pot of coffee, when Ella heard the faint jingle of the bell above the shop door. It was still locked, which meant it could only be Morgan.

"That's my daughter," she explained to Russell, whose face immediately revealed excitement.

Ella excused herself and headed down the stairs to the shop. When she rounded the corner she saw her daughter, and Emily following close behind.

They were carrying coffee cups from Bean Wild. They looked tired and disheveled, but they were giggling and goofily bumping into each other as they walked.

"Oh, hey mom," said Morgan. "What's going on? You forgot to open the shop."

"Hello sweetheart," said Ella. "Hello Emily. Are you girls okay?"

"Hi Ms. Bassett," Emily said sipping her latte. "We're good. We just, uh, stayed up too late."

"Yes, well, . . . girls, I . . .," Ella started, not sure how to explain that Emily's long-lost grandfather was sitting in her kitchen above them. "There's something I need to tell you."

"Um, okay," said Morgan with a curious smile. "Why are you being weird?"

"Emily, darling," Ella said. "This is going to be a bit of a surprise. Oh, I don't even know how to tell you this."

It quickly didn't matter how she told her, as Ella was suddenly aware that the girls were no longer looking at her. They were instead staring over her schedule. Russell Night Eagle had come downstairs without a sound, even in his dusty black cowboy boots.

"Emily," Russell said, his voice cracking.

Emily's head cocked sideways with a sly, but slightly confused grin. "Ms. Bassett, did you have a date?"

"Emily, this is Russell," Ella said.

A tear slipped loose down the man's face. "Beautiful Emily," he said, "I'm your granddad."

The End

ABOUT THE AUTHOR

B. Andrew Scott is a Chicago-based writer & producer, and host of The Sasquatch Lounge Podcast. He can also be heard regularly on ScareZone: A Halloween Horror Nights Podcast.

6-12   1-$3:30
8-10:30 +30mis

3:00 3½   6 1/2h   9½
7+2:30   9.5
                        13
                       '285
                        956
                       12250

122.56

Made in the USA
Las Vegas, NV
16 April 2021

21529298R00166